# THE LONER'S WIFE

## SMALL TOWN BACHELORS
### BOOK TWO

## SUSAN WARNER

EG PUBLISHING

This is a work of fiction. Similarities to real people, places, or events are entirely coincidental.

THE LONER'S WIFE

**First Edition. October 1, 2022.**

Copyright © 2022 EG Publishing

Print ISBN 978-1-953834-74-4

Written by Susan Warner.

If you like to get a free book from Susan Warner and would like to join her Newsletter sign up here Susan's newsletter

# CHAPTER 1

Inheritance Bay had saved Gloria Danvers's life. Okay, it wasn't like it took up arms and defended her, and it also didn't magically heal her with its "on the Bay community" feelings. But it gave her a place where she could go to recuperate. If it hadn't been for Inheritance Bay, Gloria would have still been stuck in Boston, mourning a loss that she could never get back and she would always regret.

After six months of just existing, her brother, Jack Danvers showed up, packed her condo, and brought her to Inheritance Bay. For the first month, Gloria didn't really notice she was in a different place. In fact, nothing mattered to Gloria at all. Then she began to get up and look out the window of the two-story starter home her brother lived in.

Window looking had been her concession activity that she engaged in to satisfy Jack. He wanted her to leave the house, but he was content that she had worked up to getting out of bed, getting dressed, and looking out of the window.

The only thing that broke through her depression was a little girl named Priscilla Timmons. Priscilla lived next door to Jack. Priscilla's mother, Joan Timmons, worked as the lunch matron in the school. One day, when Priscilla was on her front lawn, Gloria saw her trying to touch her toes. Priscilla just toppled over. Gloria could see the girl's form wasn't right. Most people didn't realize that yoga wasn't just relaxing, but it could also be physically challenging to do if you were a beginner.

When she saw Priscilla topple over, it was the first thing that made her think of something else besides her pain. Gloria was in a pit of despair, but she would never turn away from a child. Without giving it a second thought, she went outside to make sure Priscilla was okay.

"Are you hurt?" Gloria asked Priscilla.

Startled, the little girl yelped. Gloria stopped where she stood and held her hands in front of her.

"I'm not trying to hurt you. I saw you from the window and thought you might be hurt."

Priscilla threw back her straight black hair and blew the bangs out of her eyes.

"My mom says you are the woman whose heart is hurt, and that is why you sit at the window all day."

Gloria wasn't surprised. In a town like Inheritance Bay, any newcomer would be noticed, classified, and talked about.

"I'm Jack's sister."

"Older sister or younger sister?" Priscilla asked, looking at Gloria with curiosity.

"Younger."

Priscilla nodded. "Then it's good your brother went to get you."

Gloria wasn't so sure, but she didn't disagree with her neighbor. Trying to deflect Priscilla from digging any more into what was the shambles of her life, Gloria pointed to the ground.

"What were you trying to do?"

Priscilla just plopped to the ground. "I am in a class at school, and I have to do looking down dog."

Gloria smiled at Priscilla. It was one of the few times she had actually felt like smiling.

"You mean downward facing dog?"

Priscilla nodded, her bangs moving to and fro like a windshield wiper. "Yes, that."

"Why can't you do this move now?"

The girl looked at her feet and then let out a big sigh. "I'm fat."

Gloria looked at the young girl and wasn't sure she had heard correctly. "That can't be," Gloria exclaimed.

The girl looked up with tears shimmering in her eyes. "At school, everyone can do this but me, so the kids say I'm too fat."

Gloria looked at the girl, and for the first time in six months, she felt something. "Look, I happen to know how to do yoga. I can show you how to do this move. You are very close, and you're not fat," Gloria reassured her.

Priscilla looked hopeful, and it was that day that Gloria found her purpose. She decided she'd be a yoga teacher for school-age kids. After that event, Gloria found a part-time job at the school, working as a teaching assistant. During the next six months, she got certified as a yoga instructor for kids. Everything seemed to be in place until she decided to open a yoga school. She had been so deep in her despair that she had left all of her finances as they were. Probably not the best option when they were still entwined with a partner who thought they could still be together.

Davis was another issue. The day she left Davis, he made it very clear that their relationship was about being a power couple and making partner in the firm they both worked in. When she went to access her finances to build her school, there was a hold on them, and she had no doubt about who had put them there.

Her only other option besides using her savings account was to look at her long-term investments. A lot of her money was in long-term investments that if she took out too soon, she might pay more in taxes than she could afford. She tried to call Davis with the hope he'd be reasonable. Again, that was a sure sign she'd been in Inheritance Bay too long. Davis had no problem discussing the issue, upon Gloria's return back to Boston. The account was in both of their names. Gloria thought they would split fifty-fifty, but Davis said his expenses were much higher after she abandoned him, and he would need seventy-five percent of the fund. He reiterated that he would release the funds if she would come back to Boston and to the finance firm. The leave she had taken was indefinite because the firm knew how well she worked, but it wouldn't last forever.

Gloria had broken up with Davis three years ago. She had taken the leave a year after they split. Davis had summarily ignored her decision that they were over as a couple. His thought was that as a couple, their financial power was too much to walk away from.

When Gloria told Jack she had made up her mind to own a business and teach yoga, he had been nothing but supportive. When she had told Davis, he said they would have to settle the money issue in court. Miraculously, they couldn't get a court date that wasn't less than a year out. Gloria knew that had a lot to do with Davis having connections in high places.

So much for wanting to support a loved one, Gloria thought. That was how she found herself sitting in the perfect town of Inheritance Bay with less than a week to come up with 150k or a bank loan for the amount. At this point, neither one of them seemed likely.

When Portia called and said she had an idea, Gloria was nervous because Portia wouldn't tell her a thing about this idea. Instead, Portia asked her to meet up for brunch on a Saturday. Now, there was no doubt that Portia had been a help beyond words, but this type of ambiguity was setting Gloria's senses on alert. It was Portia, someone she trusted. It wasn't like she was Davis, but still, Gloria was uneasy with the cloak and dagger.

To be honest, Gloria could probably attest her feelings to the impromptu fundraiser Portia organized by Grayson Chance. Two things bothered her about the fundraiser. The first thing was she wished Portia would have asked her first. The second was she didn't like being in the spotlight. Gloria hated having to go to the fundraiser and pitch people. It was too much like her old life in finance, always pitching a deal. Gloria was disturbed by how easy it was for her to able to pitch her cause with ease. She could feel herself sliding back into that role as if she had never left. Selling investors on the idea of a yoga studio for kids wasn't as easy as selling investors on the idea that she could triple their money in six months with a hot tip she had.

The good part was, she would never have to see Grayson Chance again. Gloria was sure Portia would come with her upbeat attitude because she wasn't ready to admit defeat, but Gloria was close to admitting defeat and calling Davis. Just the thought of reaching out to Davis made her skin crawl. Davis wasn't a bad person—just not the one for her. Right now, the only thing Davis could think about was getting her back in Boston. Lately, Gloria was thinking about going back to Boston for a short while, until she had the money to open her studio. It wasn't her best plan, but it was better than no plan— barely. Gloria had to admit it all made her open to whatever Portia planned.

"Gloria!" Portia called out, and she looked relieved as if she hadn't expected Gloria to show. Gloria had to work on hiding her emotions better if she was so transparent that Portia doubted she would come to the breakfast. While Portia waved to her, every other man had to politely take a second look at an oblivious Portia. Gloria smiled back and shook her head. With bouncy sable hair and an air of perkiness that emanated from her, Portia was hard not to notice.

Gloria stood up and hugged Portia. A carafe of orange juice and some biscuits were on the table.

"I think it's refreshing that the place gives you

real butter and some fattening foods for the world that wants to enjoy their days instead of counting calories," Gloria said as she gestured for Portia to take a seat.

"Are we having the farmer's special today?" Portia asked.

Anyone who knew Gloria knew she loved to eat. When Portia made the suggestion, it actually relaxed Gloria. Gloria never felt like she had to put up pretense around Portia, and that was just one more thing she liked about being around Portia.

"You got here first. Were you eager to see me?" Portia asked as she settled the napkin on her lap.

"I'm always anxious to see you. I like you, Portia. You are what you say you are, and I feel totally comfortable," Gloria said with a smile.

"I'm surprised you didn't meet a nice guy at the fundraiser with cool lines like that," Portia said with a nervous laugh.

"Meet a guy while I'm going through this? The last thing I'm looking to do is meet anyone." Gloria sighed. Just thinking about the opposite sex brought visions of Davis to her mind. Nope, she wasn't interested. Gloria was a firm believer now that men and women were from different planets, and they didn't speak the same language.

"I'm not saying that the event was for meeting a guy, but there were a lot of guys who were interested in you," Portia said, wiggling her eyebrows.

"Well, they need to be interested in me—and helping me setup a yoga studio for kids," Gloria said as she slathered butter onto a biscuit.

"You know I admire your focus to start over and get the studio up, but don't you ever wish for …."

Gloria put her biscuit down and looked at Portia. One of the things she thought was such an oddity about Portia was her optimism.

"Are you asking me if I miss being in a relationship? The answer would be a firm no. Besides, I realized that before I can be in a relationship with someone else, I need to be okay with being in a relationship with myself. I never met a man who wanted to know me. I've told you about Davis. He wanted to know what I could do for him but not about me. So, now I'm doing me for dinner, me for a spa day, and me to cuddle with me."

Portia laughed. "If you spent any more time with yourself, we'd all think you had gotten married to yourself and were on a perpetual honeymoon."

"Ha, ha," Gloria said sarcastically.

Gloria heard Portia, but Gloria knew she was still a hot mess. She wouldn't want to bring a man into her life who would have to deal with her past and Davis. It wouldn't be fair to the guy.

"Anyway, Grayson said the fundraising party went really well. He was really impressed with you. He said a lot of people commented on your professional demeanor and the way you were able to handle the explanations regarding money," Portia praised.

"They weren't so impressed that they decided to invest in me," Gloria said, feeling frustrated.

"I think that Grayson may be able to still help us," Portia said expectantly.

Gloria wasn't sure what Portia thought Grayson could do, but she was out of options.

"I'm not sure what Grayson can do at this point, but I'd be willing to hear whatever he had to say."

Portia put her plate on the side, and she folded her hands in front of her on the table.

"I'm so glad that you're so open because he'll be here in a minute."

"Excuse me?" Gloria looked at Portia as if she'd lost her mind. Gloria took a quick inventory of her appearance. Her hair was in a high ponytail. She had on her stressed jeans and her black sneakers that had paint stains on them. She wasn't even going to think about the college t-shirt she had on.

"Please tell me that you're kidding, Portia," Gloria whispered.

"Sorry, I'm not. Remember, this is about the studio, not about being mad at Portia. Grayson is looking for help for one of his brothers."

"His brother wants private yoga sessions?"

Portia's smile became twice as large, and she stood up to wave to someone behind her. Gloria hoped that wasn't really Grayson, but one quick look over her shoulder confirmed it was.

"No, his brother doesn't need yoga sessions. His brother needs a financial planner. Before you decide there is a definite no, I want you to hear him out since he's here. His brother needs a lot of help, and Grayson needed someone he could trust."

Gloria slumped in the chair and looked in disbelief at Portia. "How could you tell him I'd even consider this?"

"How could I not! Your future and all of your dreams are hanging in the wind. Isn't the yoga studio and the kids worth it, or did I misunderstand how committed you were to this project?"

Gloria pulled on the fake smile and schooled her features to look engaged. In truth, this was the problem. No matter how far Gloria seemed to try to get away from it, she was always being pulled back into the finance world and its games. That was the world that had taken something from her it could never replace. Gloria fortified herself. She'd listen to Grayson and smile accordingly and then send him to Davis as a consolation prize. Maybe the gift would be enough to get him to agree to release her funds. No matter what Grayson said, there was no way she'd do this.

Grayson Chance was eye candy at any age. He was five-foot-ten with dark wavy hair and a smile that made everyone feel like a long-lost friend.

"Gloria, it's good to see you again," Grayson said cheerfully.

"Sorry for the dress down, but Portia just told me you were coming."

Grayson grinned at Portia. "I guess this meeting wasn't as planned as I thought it was. While we were doing the fundraising, I was telling Portia how my brother is an entrepreneur. He finds startups, early invests, and sometimes if he likes the company, keeps ten percent here and there. It used to be that I would look at his investments and books every quarter, but my brother has been busy this last year and his investments have tripled. I don't know if you are aware, but I'm engaged to Rose Sallow. Which means I'm being trained by Rose's twins on all the things I need to know while we plan for the wedding."

A happy couple, twins, and a wedding; there was no way that Gloria would be able to help him. Could she really stand looking at all the things she would never have? It was true she told Portia she wasn't looking for a relationship, but that didn't mean she had completely let her dreams go. Gloria looked at Portia, who was still smiling. Gloria discreetly kicked Portia under the table, and Portia reached out to pat her hand.

"I don't know if I can help you," Gloria said candidly.

"Well, it's not really me that needs the help. It's my brother, Reid."

Gloria glanced at Portia and then back at Grayson. She could see that neither one of them was going to make this easy for her.

"Listen, I hear you, but I just think that maybe you could find somebody else who would be better. On top of everything else, you know that I'm really dedicated to getting my studio up and running. I just don't see how there would be time—"

Grayson held up his hand. "I know, I know what you're going to say. Portia was clear when she said that you never do financial work, and that it's no longer even in your future plans. I'm going to be just as honest with you as Portia was with me. I want to make sure that my brother doesn't get taken advantage of, and frankly, he's away too often on his entrepreneurial whatevers in order to make sure that doesn't happen. I don't want you to stay with him forever. I just want you to get him set up so that he can have a plan—at least that he can give to someone to help him manage his finances. I'd also want you to go to maybe one or two of the places that have come up recently just to look at them to make sure that they are sound investments before you hand it off."

"Grayson, I know a lot of competent financial planners."

Just then, the waiter showed up and delivered the morning specials to everyone. Grayson and Gloria both looked at Portia.

"You were both talking, and we have to eat," Portia said, trying to defend her action of ordering the special for everyone.

Gloria stared at Portia and thought this was probably the only time someone had bought her breakfast and the last thing on her mind was the food before her. Gloria felt really bad for Grayson. He seemed like he wanted to do right by his brother. She also knew that Portia was trying to help, but neither one of them understood why she had walked away from finance. But if there were some small slivers of hope that her going back to finance would help her to get her studio, she might do it. Right now, for Gloria, the numbers just didn't add up.

Grayson took a bite out of his omelet.

"Listen, Gloria, I know that money is an issue, and I want you to know that I can go ahead and pay for the time you'll be helping my brother."

Gloria heard the words coming out of his mouth but knew he didn't really understand the kind of money she needed. He had done the fundraiser, but he had let her negotiate the amount with funders. Gloria was very impressed with the people who came to his fundraiser, but she still didn't think he understood what she was looking for to get her business up and to have three years of financing in the bank. Then she thought about what it would mean to have to go ahead and go over financial planning every day with his brother and try not to remember all the reasons why she had left her old profession—she wasn't sure she could do that.

Gloria's strategy was pretty simple. All of this could come to it amicable stop if she just gave him a number that there was no way that he could meet. She didn't have to wonder what that number was. She could give him the number that she'd been looking for the last month and then fifty percent on top of that.

"What kind of investments does he have?" she asked, hoping to get some pertinent details to give to Davis.

"He has domestic and international accounts. I'd like for him to have a plan that he understands but one he can hand to someone else, if need be, but still be aware of the schedule," Grayson said. "I'll admit, it's hard to pin Reid down and even harder when you're his brother. I'm open to getting a copy of the plan when it's done, but I need to get him to see it and be a part of the process without me present every step of the way."

"That seems like a win-win situation so you'll know someone will benefit from the work you do," Portia said. Gloria wasn't sure if she wanted to agree with her or strangle her.

"Grayson, I was serious when I told you I know someone who can do this for you."

Grayson nodded sagely and pushed his plate aside while he folded his hands in front of him.

"Well, let's get to the heart of the matter then. How about I offer you 250,000, and you take care of everything?

That was when Gloria looked at Portia and asked,

"Is he for real?"

Portia smiled and nodded. Gloria faced Grayson and pasted on a smile.

"If the number holds, and I can get fifty percent upfront, you've got a deal."

Grayson smiled. "I can deliver it to you by five today. I know where you live so I'm not worried about flight risk." With that, Grayson pulled his plate in front of him and ate with gusto. Gloria wouldn't even be able to remember what was on her plate, just that she was going back to the fire.

# CHAPTER 2

*I*t was the first week of October, also known as quarterly torture week. Reid was hoping, since he had seen his brother less than two weeks ago, that maybe he wouldn't have to see him again in order to go over his finances. He should have known better. What made it worse was now that Grayson had fallen in love with Rose, he wasn't going to be able to stay with his brother either. So much for him telling his brother his tales of adventure.

"Reid, you were at the wrong terminal," Grayson said as he engulfed his brother in a hug. He couldn't tell Grayson that he had wanted to get himself to the office. He needed time to adjust to his brother not being there for him whenever he needed him. No one said it, but all the brothers knew Grayson was the rock they all depended on.

Grayson's new office building was a couple of blocks away from Momma Patti's house. Reid knew why Grayson had gotten it. He didn't want to be too far from home now that he was preparing the nest for him, Rose, and the twins. However, as Reid looked around, he could tell this was smaller than any other office Grayson had owned.

"You didn't really think I was going to take a commercial flight, did you?" Reid joked with his brother. "That being in love thing must really be all-encompassing. The last time I took a commercial flight, I think it was when I originally came to Inheritance Bay when I was five."

"There's nothing wrong with taking a commercial flight," argued Grayson.

"No, there isn't. I just want to get where I'm going now and not later," Reid said as he looked around the office, trying to find some redeemable quality about it. He dropped his bag and jacket on a nearby wooden chair. When the chair rocked after he laid his jacket on it, he hoped it would stay in one piece. Then he stood his luggage next to the nearby desk and was relieved when that didn't wobble as well.

Grayson took a seat and sighed, looking at his brother.

"I'm so happy to see that you're all in one piece and not sporting a cast."

Reid waved off Grayson's concerns.

"I haven't been in the cast in a very long time. I mean, if we think about it, the last time I was in a cast must have been what... two years ago," Reid commented as he looked around the office.

Grayson shook his head. "You tumbled down the side of the mountain."

"To be fair, I didn't tumble. It was a black trail, and my skis got tangled on the hidden root under the snow and it just ruined my trajectory," Reid defended.

"You know you're not going to be able to do this all of your life."

"I'm just making sure that I'm living my life to the fullest, that's all."

Grayson held up his hands. "I'm not here to talk to you about your lifestyle. That is on you."

"I'm glad."

"However, I would be remiss as your brother and financial advisor to not bring up the idea that doing these excursions makes your insurance policy a beast of a premium."

Reid sat back in the chair.

"Are you trying to tell me that I'm going broke, and I might have to get a nine to five job?" Reid joked.

"I would if I thought it would stop you from testing everything. There has to be an end to it," Grayson said, concerned. Reid hated it when he worried Grayson, but he wasn't like Grayson. Reid harbored no dreams of finding that special woman.

"It's not a phase, and I want you to know, for someone who isn't going to have that discussion, this really feels like we are having that discussion," Reid said with a smile.

"Sorry, sorry, I'm your brother, and I'm worried," Grayson said.

"I don't have a death wish. I just want to make sure I did it all. Speaking of doing it all. I just want to confirm, why are we sitting in this office space when we haven't bought the building and renovated it?"

"I'm a fundraiser, Reid. Sometimes I hit all of the right buttons and it rains, but most times it just trickles money, so I can't go around in my own jet," he said solemnly.

"What?" Do you need cash? You know it's not even a question. You know where all of my money is. Please go ahead and take what you need," Reid offered.

Grayson sat back in the rickety chair, and Reid waited to hear if his big brother was in trouble. Had he missed some of the signs that Grayson was having money problems? When he and Vincent came for dinner, there weren't any signs that he could think of. Grayson's weight still looked good. He was still dressing in tailored clothing.

"And if I did need a significant part of your fortune?" Grayson asked in a low voice.

"I can make money. Take what you need, and I'll do the rest. I have new investments coming in, and I've stashed some pockets of quick cash that I can get to today, if you need it. Besides, with Kathy by my side, we can find some ripe companies to pluck up before anyone realizes the hidden gems they are and get some quick cashflow."

Grayson reached out his hand, and Reid grabbed it. "You're an amazing brother, Reid. I'm good. My money is better. I bought this spot more for Rose than anything else."

"Ah, yes. Rose, she who can make you forget your rules and turn over a new …. petal maybe?" Reid said, trying to lighten the mood.

Grayson laughed off the joke. "I have news."

Reid moved out of his chair and fell to one knee.

"Is it from the petal goddess who has bespelled you? Tell me about the fair maiden who has taken your heart. I wait with bated breath to find out what golden nuggets of wisdom have fallen from her tongue," Reid professed on bended knee.

"Get up, silly. I'm going to be doing a new fundraiser for a new company. They are very small, and they will be looking for someone to hold their hand into corporate."

Reid got up from the floor and sat in the nearby chair.

"You should have told me this was about money, brother. I may test the items and manage money. When it comes to adopting companies and guiding them to profitability, I leave that to Kathy. However, I'm not above being the messenger boy to her," Reid said with a grin.

"It's a couple of women who have made an invention called water pots. You put a plant in it, and the pot changes color to say when you need to water it or don't. They make pots for four types of plants right now, and they are on backorder and sold out of most of their inventory."

Reid heard the idea and knew right away that Kathy would love it. Kathy was his biological younger sister. She hadn't been so fortunate in the foster care system, but as soon as Reid was old enough, he went looking for her. He didn't probe, but she didn't like to go out, she had no friends, and she loved to work in the garden. The other skill she had was being able to look at a company and tell you the path to profitability. She didn't think anything of it, but she had saved more than her fair share of jobs.

"I can't give you their data, but you and several others can come to the fundraiser," Grayson said.

Reid shook his head. "Wow, gone are the days when being kin meant a leg in," Reid complained.

"Hey, I'm telling you, so you know what is going to be there. Get your research done and come with an open wallet."

Reid slouched in the chair. "You could have told me to get in line like all of the other peasants on the phone. Why did you call me out here?"

Grayson started to fidget, and Reid knew whatever it was, it was important to him. This was the Grayson that few people saw. It was the Grayson who knew he was about to do the right thing but wasn't sure how it would be received. Reid wanted to tell him yes to whatever it was, but he had to be patient.

"You know about Rose, obviously," Grayson said. "And you know we are engaged. It won't be long before we marry."

Reid couldn't say he was surprised. He had come just a few weeks ago, and he knew then that Rose wasn't going to be a fly-by-night woman. As soon as Grayson said Momma Patti would have liked her, Reid knew it was a done deal.

"Wow, already planning on taking the big jump to marriage," Reid said as he sat up leaning closer to Grayson. "I expected the engagement—but marriage?"

Grayson nodded.

"You don't have to say anything. I can see your thoughts on your face. So let me answer those questions. I am not running to the first person that I ran into in order to have some sort of family now that Mama is gone. Rose is an amazing woman. The only reason I'm not marrying her right now is that she's the one who said we need to wait," Grayson said with a grin.

Grayson was right. Reid had been thinking those things. That Grayson was thinking everything out gave Reid a little more relief. It wasn't going to do anything for Vincent, the suspicious brother who would question Rose and ask if he could do a background check on her. He was also thinking how lucky Grayson was. Reid, on the other hand, couldn't seem to find a woman who understood his love of life. He had tried to be in several relationships, but all of them had wanted him to change. He knew he couldn't keep doing his daredevil stunts all of his life, but he wanted a woman who would accept him the way he was. He wanted a woman that was like the one Grayson had found, someone who accepted him as he was. He was happy for his brother, but Reid also hoped that Rose wasn't one-of-a-kind.

Reid tried to clear his mind. His life was fine just the way it was. He had his baby sister, money, and he was free to do whatever he wanted, alone.

"Rose is the woman I've waited for all my life, Reid," Grayson said with joy shining in his eyes. "She's got children that love me. When I'm with her, I'm not scared that some recessive gene I don't know about will surface and I'll leave. She's my best friend that I didn't know that I was missing."

"Grayson, there isn't another more deserving. Out of all of us, you have put in the time and

worked the hardest. When I tell you I'm happy for
you, I want you to know I may be thinking, 'darn it
if only I'd see her first,' but, I'm happy for you and
I'm still confused about what this has to do with me,"
Reid said.

"You know, Reid, you live every day as if
tomorrow is going to be your last one. To be frank
with you, I worry about you. I know that you and
Kathy are very good at making and finding money,
but you also have to be good at maintaining that
money. One of the things Rose is really good about,
probably because she's a single mom with kids, is
that she always knows where her money is. I raise
lots of money, but I have to tell you, I'm a little jaded
because I do. For me, more money is just a party
away, but I realize that isn't the case for everyone.
Everyone else has to manage their money
accordingly. When I marry Rose, I won't have the
time to manage all of your financial affairs. I want to
make sure that you are in good hands."

"So, the way you're talking makes it sounds like
you've taken steps and you already know whom you
would like me to talk to."

Grayson smiled.

"I think that I've found the right person to help
you. I met her during one of my fundraising events,
and I have to say, she has the type of work ethic and
drive that I think a person would need in order to get
your finances and shape and be able to hand them
over to you."

"A woman?" Reid said skeptically.

"Reid, she's not interested in you, or anyone for
that matter. It's one of the reasons why I picked her,
because she doesn't seem to want to be around any

man at all, unless he's under the age of ten and wants to learn yoga."

"A woman, though? I can tell you didn't run this by Vincent," Reid said with a grin.

Grayson shook his head.

"As soon as you say it's a woman, he's already calling his investigative team," Grayson confirmed. "He's still in town doing some last-minute looking in the boxes that mom left for us. It seems like the only time I can get the both of my brothers to see me is when I'm holding an event for a new company."

"I'll see this woman."

"Good. The other thing I want is for my brothers to try and meet Rose while you are here. I know you are always busy. Maybe while you are learning about your finances, you could make some time to meet my fiancée."

"No problem. So, when do we meet this woman whom you think can wrangle my finances?"

"I was hoping to meet her for lunch. That gives us just enough time to review some of the fundraisers I'm doing so you and Kathy can look them over. When we finish, we can meet her for lunch. It'll be tight, but I think we can do it," Grayson said.

"This whole falling in love and getting married has really turned your priorities upside down. I thought people we employ had to wait on us. We weren't racing to find them," Reid commented with a laugh.

Grayson nodded. "Well, I think that you should handle it any way you want, but remember we had to practically bribe her to take you on. Put your best foot forward."

Reid put his hands up in surrender.

"I will listen to what she has to say. I'll let her know what direction I'd like to stay in, and I'll be a good boy," Reid said with his best angelic look on.

"She's also going to evaluate two of the newest acquisitions," Grayson said matter-of-factly.

"I get it! I'll be good, okay? As long as she knows her business, I'm sure we will get along just fine."

The next two hours passed entirely too quickly. Grayson looked at his watch and reminded Reid about his lunch date. Reid had to admit he was a bit frustrated to leave his brother, but he had promised to be on his best behavior. He didn't even bother to leave his bags with Grayson. Perhaps Grayson was feeling more amenable to the opposite sex since he fell in love, but business was business. Reid didn't think the meeting would be long at all and he'd be able to get on a plane back home tonight.

He'd meet with the woman and then give her a rundown of his investments, and she'd probably run away. No reason to get a hotel room or inconvenience his brother. This would be a quick meeting.

The address was at a seafood place called the Twisted Shrimp. Reid walked in and asked the host if someone named Gloria Danvers had arrived. The host nodded toward a table, and Reid left his bags at the front door. He would be on his best behavior like he promised his brother. Besides, he would have to confess that he was curious to see this mysterious woman..

It wasn't often Reid was surprised, but the woman sitting here, waiting for him had to be a goddess from his dreams.

"Gloria Danvers?" he said with a smile and his hand out.

She looked at his hand. She didn't take it, and then looked him in the eye. "You're late. Can you give me a good reason not to leave before this starts? It looks like one of us isn't really serious."

# CHAPTER 3

*H*e was late.

A person who couldn't respect another person's time probably couldn't handle their money. This was a bad idea from the beginning. Gloria knew this wasn't where she should be anyway. It was true she needed the money, but did she really need the money this badly? Reid Chance. She was going to give him another ten minutes, and then she would leave. She was preparing to take off, and then she looked over her shoulder. There was a man at the door who was a walking dream for a sculptor. It wasn't like he was uniquely handsome, although he was the type a woman might look twice at. He had an air about him that said he knew everyone wanted to know him. Arrogance at its purest.

He had on a blue shirt that was open at the collar, flashing tanned skin. It appeared as though he had on some business slacks, but Gloria didn't want to stare to confirm her thoughts. Then the unthinkable happened. The host pointed toward her, and the mystery man began to walk in her direction.

Gloria knew that Grayson was attractive, but she didn't know what to expect from his brother. In the grand scheme of things, they weren't even really blood related. How could she have known that he would have been so stunning, and so late? Gloria started to wonder if he thought his looks gave him carte blanche in order to play hacky sack with everyone else's time.

When he finally approached her, and held out his hand, introducing himself, Gloria said what was on her mind.

"You're late. Can you give me a good reason not to leave before this starts? It looks like one of us isn't really serious."

"Forgive me, I am serious about doing this. I just got caught up spending time with Grayson because we don't see each other as much as I'd like."

How could Gloria hold it against him that he wanted to see his brother? She pulled out a book out of her briefcase and opened it up on the table. Time would tell whether or not Reid was going to be a responsible person or not.

"Well, I'm happy that you're finally here. The way I'd like to approach this is to find out what it is that you know or that you think you know about your own finances. Rose and Grayson are working on their engagement while they're simultaneously planning their wedding. It's my understanding that Grayson wants you to be up and competent before the wedding occurs. At the rate that things are moving between them right now, I think the whole town is anticipating a wedding either in December or January."

"Didn't Grayson give you a list of all of my investments?" Reid asked.

Gloria patted her black portfolio and nodded.

"Grayson is very efficient, and yes, of course, he gave me a list of all of your investments and the two properties that he would like us both to visit. However, that has nothing to do with my request. The real question here, Reid, is do you know what you have or don't you?" Gloria asked.

"I've got two new holdings. They're not producing as they should, but I give all of my acquisitions about six months to get up to speed. If the businesses don't make the cut, then my sister Kathy is sent in to fix them. I know my net worth is roughly around 8.3 million, not enough to own my own toys but enough to rent some toys without breaking my spending allowance, which never exceeds eight percent of what comes in any given month. I invest in a lot of new startups and new technologies. The place where I donate the most money to are projects that help children. Although I make sure to cap my donations at ten percent of my yearly adjusted income."

Gloria was suitably impressed. However, her features never let on and she knew her face was as bland as if he were saying the alphabet.

"I'm very happy that you're aware of your assets. I haven't met this Kathy, but I have a note here that says that she's instrumental in your investments as well."

Reid leaned across the table, bringing him closer to her than she was prepared for.

"So did I pass, and do you forgive me for being late?" he asked with a smile that threaten to pull her in and make her forget what she was thinking about.

"You pass for having a good understanding of what you have so this shouldn't be a chore

getting you on a schedule. As for being late, you're going to have to do a lot more than recite something from memory and then smile engagingly."

"So, you think my smile is engaging, you say," Reid asks as he gives her another smile and wiggles his eyebrows.

"I also think that Shar Pei's are cute dogs with an engaging smile. They have wrinkles upon wrinkles, but I would never think to have one as a pet."

"Well, I think a Shar Pei pup goes for about $750-$1500, so you think my smile is engaging and worth about $1500; I still see this as a win."

Gloria smiled.

"Fine, you win." Gloria could see the self-satisfied smile on his face as if he were the cat that had caught the mouse. The problem was that Gloria could think of many a woman who wouldn't mind being caught by Reid Chance.

"I'll be honest with you, Gloria. The only reason I know the information I know is because I get regular updates from my sister Kathy. She is the one who identifies with good prospects there are, and I'm the one who goes to test if what they're selling really works."

"Thanks for sharing that. It says a lot about your character that you acknowledge other people and their work, instead of taking credit for it," Gloria said.

"So, I guess you must run into a lot of clients who either don't know what they have or think they have more than they do? Either way, it must be pretty interesting."

"I have definitely had my fair share of trying to explain to people what their net worth really is as opposed to how much money they see coming in the door or even in their bank accounts. Money is a funny thing. You get to see the true character of a person when they have money and when they don't. It's probably because it shows their true nature that I really don't like to do this kind of personal financial planning too often. I prefer children."

"Yet here you are with me?"

"Circumstances have brought me here, not you," Gloria said with a polite smile.

For a moment, Gloria hoped that Reid didn't grill Grayson about why she was taking this job. She couldn't really explain why, but she really didn't want him to know why she was doing this. Reid getting too close and having too much information about her would put her at a disadvantage.

"Well, I'm not going to look a gift horse in the mouth. I'm glad that you're on board." Reid said with a winning smile on his face.

"So, looking at our time constraint, I want us to be able to go through the books in the next week, and then let's schedule to go to your two new properties as soon as possible."

Gloria looked up at Reid, and for a moment she could swear that he was staring at her but that would be crazy. This was just another reason this assignment was a bad idea. If she couldn't keep herself objective when she was around him, it was going to take twice as long to get him organized.

"Whatever you think is best," Reid said.

"Well, good. This should be relatively painless for us both. I'll look at some projections, then get us a working plan."

Reid laughed. "In business and in most investments, a plan is just a general outline."

Gloria shook her head. "I disagree that a plan is just a general outline. If your plan becomes an outline, it's because you haven't made decisions or you're not sticking with the ones that you claim to have already made. By staying firm to the path, you are guaranteed to get the outcome that you planned for."

"And if the environment changes in the business world?" Reid queried.

"I think that you need to make a decision about the business world as well as about life. You have to focus on an end goal and then put everything you have toward it. Of course, there may be some exceptions to the rule where the thing you're looking for becomes obsolete. However, barring that occurrence, you make a plan, you do the steps, you do the research, and you stick to it."

Reid looked as if he'd just been slapped.

"So, I guess I'm a little confused here. You work in finance, where things change by the minute. Finance people are always looking at a little ticker tape on a television screen trying to figure out if they still have the money they woke up to that morning. You don't find there's any variability in that? You think that we should make a plan and stick to it?"

Gloria smiled. "The trick to that little ticker tape

on the screen is that it's only for people who aren't in it for the long game. If you're trying to make short money or if you're going to be a day trader, then please look at the little ticker tape. However, history is clear. Cycles may come and go, and dips may be lower than normal. Highs may be higher than what you expected, but in the end, staying firm and on the course will make you a profit better than what you came in with."

"Is that your theory with life and finances?"

"In my world, Reid, life is finances, and the answer to that would be yes, safe is always better." Gloria thought things were going well and that she and Reid understood each other. However, after hearing him flout the idea of rules and plans, Gloria had to review her impression of Reid. Gloria understood how people like Reid lived. They pushed and pushed and thought the ends justified the means. They believed in living today even if it could put tomorrow in jeopardy. That type of life theory was great until you had something to lose. Some things—when you lost them—there was no way to get them back.

"If you are looking for a plan that will find ways to predict new trends. I'm not the person for you."

"I'm not asking for a genie, but I'm not opposed to speculation," Reid said.

"How much is okay to lose during speculation?" Gloria asked.

Reid shrugged. "I don't know no more than twenty-eight percent of what you invested."

Gloria knew they were in different ballparks. She spoke in dollars, and he spoke in percentages.

"You mean twenty-eight dollars?" Gloria prodded.

He stopped, and his mouth opened and closed like a fish out of water. Seeing him off-kilter and acting normal was kind of fun.

"Please tell me you mean twenty-eight dollars on the hundred," Reid said in a strangled voice.

Gloria smiled and shook her head. Then the waiter interrupted and brought the appetizers and drinks she had pre-ordered for the meeting. Once again, she could see that Reid wasn't used to not controlling the situation.

"Is there a problem with the selection and beverage? I can get you something else," Gloria offered.

Reid shook his head. "It's not that. I usually order and did you pay for this? You know I'm paying for this right so—"

Gloria held up her hand. "I'm paying because this is my meeting to decide if we can work together or not."

Reid stopped cold and looked at Gloria as if she had sprouted two heads.

"Is there a problem, Reid?" Gloria asked in a sweet voice.

"You're not sure you want to work with me?" he asked incredulously and hurt all at the same time.

"We've got the appetizers and the beverages for me to make a final decision," Gloria said.

Reid nodded. "So, if you decided to work with me this will all be done, written up and delivered by…"

"Thanksgiving. I can meet you before or after so

as to not interfere with any personal plans you may have."

"No, no personal plans that I know of. However, every year, Kathy tries to hold an event for the employees that I attend. I'm not with anyone, and I suppose Grayson will be with Rose this year."

Gloria noted his words, not that she cared who he was or wasn't with. For the life of her, she couldn't explain why she had told Reid she was still thinking about working with him when the money had already been wired and was waiting for her acceptance. The fact that he wasn't seeing anyone wasn't a concern for her at all. Reid's social life had no bearing on Gloria's decision. She was just trying to be considerate of his social situation.

After taking a sip of her club soda, Gloria decided to put Reid out of his misery.

"I'm going to take this assignment, Reid."

"Are you sure?" Reid asked.

Gloria felt like there was more to his question, but she nodded anyway.

Reid smiled that thousand-watt smile, and Gloria knew she was in trouble.

# CHAPTER 4

"Now that we're partners, let me apologize. I was so overcome by your confidence and beauty I acted like an elementary kid. I stuttered and wanted to tug your braid. Will you let me make it up to you?" Reid said, gauging her reaction and hoping he hadn't read Gloria wrong.

"I'm listening."

"Hello, my name is Reid Chance. I'm Grayson's brother, and I happen to make my money by helping other people fulfill their dreams. I was adopted by Pattie Chance, hence the last name, and I was fortunate enough to find the only blood relative I have—Kathy. When I brought Kathy to Momma Patti, she took her under her wing as well. Grayson is going to get married and live the happily ever after Momma Patti told us someone was out there for us all. However, Grayson being Grayson wants to make sure that I'm okay. I'd appreciate it if you could help ease his mind."

Gloria smiled, and Reid wanted to fall at her feet. Maybe it was her hair that was uncommonly long for this day and age. Gloria had sable brown tresses, that were braided and then wrapped in a circle like a bun. However, the bun was so heavy it hung low near the nape of her neck. The only thing Reid could think about was how he really wanted to know how long her hair truly was.

It was her smile that prompted Reid to hold out his hand. When Gloria took it, he felt her slender digits slide into his. As his hand wrapped around hers, he thought of the contradiction she was. She was delicate but strong enough to stand up to him. Reid was nowhere near ready to let her hand go when he felt her hand retreat. Reluctantly, he let her hand go. How would it look for him to hold on just as he was trying to convince her that he was a good guy?

This woman was anti-all that he has ever said about life and finance, but his heart has never skipped a beat around another woman. Reid knew he was going to have to take this opportunity of working with her as a way to get to know her. He needed to figure out what was this attraction he had to her and if it was just a passing thing.

"If you could give me your schedule, then I'll be able to look at what I have to do on mine and then make some arrangements so we can go and look at your other two acquired investments," Gloria said.

"I've got a better idea. Why don't you tell me what days work best for you, and I'll make myself available because you're doing me the favor," he said.

Once again, he could see he had taken her by surprise. If it wasn't so childish, he would have stood up in the middle of the restaurant and fist pumped into the middle of the air. The appetizers were almost gone, and Reid was in no hurry to leave. He signaled to the waiter to refill his glass. It was the only time he could remember asking for seltzer water. Right now, it didn't matter what was in the glass, as long as it kept Gloria with him for a little longer.

"Us going somewhere sounds suspiciously like a date, considering I'm a big girl and I can do financial assessments in my sleep."

"I don't want you to think of this as a date. When I pick new investments, it's not just numbers. I want to show you what I see. Just outside of Inheritance Bay there is a place called Heaven's Gate. It's off the beaten path, but it's set up like a resort. It's run by Petr Kozlov."

"You can introduce me, and I'll go through the property and…"

"No, it's fine. It'll be the first time I go through it with a woman, and I'd be interested in your insight."

"I thought you said that Kathy oversees the new businesses," Gloria said.

Reid didn't want to get into it about his sister, but it was going to come up eventually.

"Kathy comes in when the property isn't doing well. She can make anything profitable."

"Are you trying to tell me that Kathy has the Midas touch, and you're the brawn in this situation?"

"What I'm trying to say is that when Kathy looks at the numbers, if it all works out well and she says there's a path to profitability, we do whatever she says."

Gloria smiled. "So, you're looking out for everybody's interest, is that right?"

Reid snapped his fingers and winked at her.

"See, I knew you would understand exactly what my role is here."

Gloria flipped through her black book and then looked back up at Reid.

"It says that you have some property in the mountains?"

"Yes, I do."

"Can I expect you'll be joining me at that location as well?"

Reid spread his hands trying to affect an innocent look.

"I want to be around as much as possible to understand how you are evaluating my assets," Reid said with a smile.

Gloria choked on the club soda she was drinking.

"Let's be clear. I'm here to look at the assets listed on this spreadsheet and nothing more."

"Maybe I need to update the spreadsheet," Reid said.

Gloria shook her head. "I have a better idea. Why don't I plan out how this will be, and then I'll let you know if I think you're needed or not? I can't see myself inconveniencing you if it's not necessary."

"Gloria, we have to trust each other. If I already have the means, I think it would be easier if we went together. Now I have two sites—one I just purchased and one I've had for a year. One is in Windham, NY and the other is Montauk."

"Montauk; on the tip of the Long Island, correct?" Gloria asked.

Reid nodded sheepishly. "Yes, there's one there

because I thought Kathy would visit so I brought some machines to recreate a winter wonderland, but she never visited and I'm still hoping. I keep asking her to visit, and she keeps saying no," Reid said.

"Do you think she wants to come to the evaluation with us? Since its business?" Gloria stressed.

Reid could see he had walked into that one, and he handled it with the aplomb of a veteran. "I'll ask her now."

*HEY, SUNFLOWER, DID YOU WANT TO TAKE A RUN TO MONTAUK AND SEE HOW THE SUN FEELS ON A MOUNTAINTOP?*

Reid didn't have to wait long before Kathy answered. It didn't give him nearly enough time to look at Gloria.

*IS THERE A PROBLEM? I LOOKED AT LAST QUARTER. IT WAS LOW BUT NOT ENOUGH TO CAUSE AN ALARM. IS SOMETHING OFF?*

*NO JUST SEEING IF THOSE ROOTS OF YOURS WOULD LIKE NEW SOIL.*

*PLANTS DON'T WALK BUT THANK YOU.*

"We're good to do Montauk," Reid confirmed. Reid watched Gloria diligently write in her little black book, and he had to admit he was a little curious about the book.

"You've got that look about you, so let me satisfy that curiosity I see now. I just keep my notes in it."

Reid held up his hands. "I was just looking."

"You were just looking like my friend Portia was looking. I have to tell you she was very disappointed, and you will be too if you are expecting something juicy in this binder," Gloria warned.

"So, you're not going to give me any hints at all

on yourself? I'm saying I could be feeling a bit vulnerable with you knowing so much about me, and I don't know a thing about you," Reid said innocently.

Gloria smiled. "Reid, you seem like a nice guy, despite the way this started, but I'm not looking for anyone."

Reid nodded. "I get you're not looking for anyone right now. I'd just like to be your friend. Until you come to the conclusion that I'm obviously the best guy around."

"Confident, aren't you?"

"The only one who could have beat me out is Grayson, and he's getting married to the love of his life," Reid said.

"Fine. I'll let you make the arrangements, so we can go to Montauk. In order for me to evaluate the workflows, we're going to have to run through all of the facility. This may be a tedious day for you because I'm detailed."

"You won't even know I'm there," Reid said, zipping his mouth and throwing away the key.

"Somehow, I highly doubt that. Let me just send a text to Grayson so he'll know."

Reid wanted to tell her that Grayson would be okay with whatever they decided, but he knew now she was a by-the-book-and-plan kind of woman.

"Well, Mr. Chance, it seems as though everything is in order, and your brother has approved you doing the arrangements. Now, I need to get going."

Reid stood up. "You can't leave now. The appetizers and drinks aren't done."

Gloria smiled. "Well, normally I don't leave until they are gone, but you were late and so I'm sure you'll understand how I need to get to my next appointment."

With that, Gloria stood up and walked out of the restaurant and Reid watched her as she left. Gloria Danvers was a woman like no other. He had never met a woman like her and until he knew what was going on he wasn't going to let her go.

Later that day, Reid took a limo to get back home to Westchester where Kathy, his sister, waited for him. After being around Gloria, he felt a bit pretentious taking the jet for such a short hop. As the car rocked him to sleep, his thoughts drifted to Gloria. She wasn't what he expected. She might need a plan for everything, but Reid knew great discoveries could happen spontaneously. The car stopped, and he looked out the window at the familiar scene of Westchester. Like clockwork, Kathy was at the door when Reid got out of the car.

"Kathy, I don't have any seeds to give you, forgive me," he said dramatically as he approached her

Reid's sister stood at the door with her arms crossed over her chest and smudges of dirt on her cheeks. It told Reid she'd been in the greenhouse and hadn't left the house today. Reid tried not to let his disappointment show, but Kathy seemed to read body signals so well he wasn't sure that he'd succeeded.

"You missed the quarterly review this afternoon. I took care of it, but I just wanted you to know. The board wasn't sure if you were injured or late. When I told them you weren't injured, they suggested I needed to keep better tabs on you."

Reid pulled Kathy into his embrace. A lot of people would overlook her quiet demeanor, but she'd survived more than most. She wouldn't tell Reid everything, but what he knew was enough to make sure no one ever bothered her again.

"Thanks for covering, and for the record, they are your board too."

"What did Grayson want?"

Reid walked Kathy into the house to sit on the couch. He knew she harbored a secret fear that Grayson would one day dislike her for one reason or another and force him to choose between them. He had tried to allay her fears. First, Grayson wasn't that kind of person, and second, if Reid had to choose, he would never leave Kathy.

"My brother has gone and fallen in love."

"That's great!"

"Going to dedicate all of his time to his life. He wants to make sure that I'm in total control of mine."

Kathy looked at him, and she was still confused.

"What I'm trying to say is that Grayson hired a woman to review my finances and give me a write-up on what I have and what I don't have."

Kathy gave him a long, hard look, and then she just turned away and started laughing. He knew what her reaction was going to be and there was no way to get around it.

"So let me get this straight. Your brother hired a stranger to educate you about your books?"

"Yes, Kathy, it's not funny. Had it been anyone else, I'd be offended."

"You know, I've been telling you for a very long time that everyone underestimates you because of the way you act."

"Not you too, Kathy. I just living my life to the fullest."

"At that rate, you're probably living your life the most foolishly," she quipped back.

"Okay, sunflower, that's enough."

"It must be very nice that you know that he cares so much about you." S

he sighed.

"I guess it is, but it's also aggravating to think that he doesn't think I know how to handle my finances."

"I'm sure he believes in you. He's just been taking care of you for a very long time. I think it wouldn't make a lot of sense if he stopped now."

Reid thought about what she said and then watched her look everywhere but at him.

"What's on your mind, sunflower?"

"You think they'll invite me to the wedding?"

"I don't have to wonder. My brother will invite us both, and you will sit on the side of the groom as honored family."

Reid watched as she tried to blink back the tears of happiness.

"You know, Grayson's wife fancies that she can match up anyone who is single. If you stay in this house, you will be a sitting duck for her."

Kathy rolled her eyes and pushed him away from her. "I'll be in the greenhouse. If she sends anyone, I'll tell them I'm the gardener," she said with a laugh.

"You should be out and about, Kathy," he said in a low voice filled with concern.

"It's the cold part of the year. You know that I prefer the atmosphere of the greenhouse."

"I could make paths of heaters so that you would go outside."

"You know, you tend to go down this path when you are avoiding something. What firm did he hire to help you?"

"So, you aren't open to the path of warmth made just for you?"

"Reid?" she said, dragging his name out.

"He didn't hire a firm."

"Well, I suppose one person could do it. Who is he? Father time that Grayson hired?"

"No. So I'm going to say this, and then I need you to let it go."

"Okay."

"He hired a woman." Kathy turned and sat back next to Reid.

"An attractive woman."

"Yes!"

"Don't read too much into this. She doesn't want anything to do with me."

Kathy got up and sashayed to the exit. "I know you think you are very slick, but I heard you, brother. She may not want anything to do with you, but you definitely want to do something with her."

Reid got up and followed her. "No, Kathy, listen. You don't understand.... "

Hanna and Anna Sallow had a daddy, and they were going to school. Hanna had on all of her new clothes that Grayson had helped her buy. It was going to be great. Her mom was doing some work, but Grayson was taking them to school just like all the other parents. Moms came all the time, but when a dad showed up, everyone noticed.

Last month, Hanna's mom, Rose, met Grayson, and now he was a daddy in training. Her mom, Rose, told the twins, to celebrate them being together, they were going to do dress up around Thanksgiving in front of all of their friends.

Hanna couldn't wait. She loved to dress up.

"Hey, gals. Are you two okay? Do you need me to go in with you?"

Hanna really like Grayson. He was learning how to be a daddy, and so far, he was good at remembering things.

"No, we can go in by ourselves, thank you."

"I know you don't need it, Hanna, but I'd like to meet the teacher first, okay?"

"Okay."

A tall woman came up to them and smiled. She bent down so she was the same height as Hanna and Anna.

"Hello, young ladies. I'm Ms. Litkin. I teach pre-k and Kindergarten."

Hanna immediately took the initiative.

"I'm Hanna Sallow, and this is my sister Anna Sallow, and this is our new dad, Grayson Chance. He's not officially our new dad until thanksgiving so he's like a dad in training"

Ms. Litkin was very nice, and then she stood up and looked at Grayson

"Hello, Dad in training," she said with a smile.

"Hi."

"So, the process is we collect the children here in the morning and bring them back in the afternoon."

"Great, so you will be their teacher," Grayson asked

"I will be for one of them," she said.

Hanna turned to look at Ms. Litkin. "One of us? "Anna said, nervous.

Ms. Litkin bent down again. "We want to make sure you get to make your own friends, and everyone knows you, so you will be put in two separate classes.

Grayson said it was a good idea, and Anna and Hanna looked at one another, unsure.

Grayson bent down. "Remember, we try new things, right?"

The twins nodded.

"We don't say yuck until we've given it a chance, right?"

The twins nodded.

"Okay, let's give it a try and see how it goes."

Grayson left, and Hanna nodded but she wasn't sure this was a good idea at all.

# CHAPTER 5

*K*athy Ellis had a smile on her face, but her mind was wondering where her go bag was. Kathy knew that this day would come. Her brother tried to do the very best for her, and she couldn't have asked for a better person. They had been separated when they were younger into separate adoption agencies. He had found her and brought her into his life. It was after he had given her an education that she found out she could help companies grow from in the red to profitable. Not all of them were worth the work, but she could always see the path to wholeness.

It wasn't like she didn't believe that her brother loved her. However, Kathy had grown up in places where she understood that sometimes love just wasn't enough. When he had missed the meeting, her first thought was there was something wrong with him or maybe he was hurt. He had this ridiculous rule to always test all the products. She had thought that maybe he finally got his comeuppance and there was a product that had tested him to his limit.

Now that he was home, safe and sound, Kathy knew what had made him forget his business obligations: a woman. Reid couldn't see it, but Kathy did. The fact that he was following her to straighten out any misconceptions she might have was all the information she needed.

"I was wondering if this new woman has any connection to you wanting to go to Montauk all of a sudden?" Kathy asked as they fixed themselves a coffee in the kitchen.

"You said you didn't want to go," Reid replied.

"I don't, but my curiosity was piqued when Petr called. He said he wanted to make sure you weren't coming to tell him that you were going to take away his funding."

"So, I'm the bad guy, or is it that he has a thing for you?"

Kathy waved Reid off. She didn't think she'd ever be ready to be in a relationship, but Reid didn't want to give up hope. Reid had been the lucky kid. She'd never found a foster home that was anything a child should be in. Kathy knew it hadn't been as bad as some of the people she knew, but it was enough for her to know that love was fickle, and she wanted no part of it.

"You can try to change the subject if you want, but it's not going to work. Now, tell me about the woman who wants nothing to do with the man who has it all," she said, looking at Reid. She watched him squirm under her gaze as he tried to pass this new woman as nothing special.

"I'm going to call Petr and let him know I'm not

yanking his funding. I'm just bringing out a consultant to look the place over."

Kathy laughed. "Oh yeah, that is going to make him feel so much better."

Reid held his hands up. "Okay, you call him and tell him he's not in trouble. I'm just coming to look with a business associate."

Kathy picked up the phone and called Petr. She knew all things eventually come to an end. Kathy was the type of person who didn't like surprises.

"Hello, Petr, its Kathy. I wanted to talk to you about Reid's visit." Kathy spoke to Petr, and he was happy that she called. Just as Kathy was winding down, Reid tapped her on her shoulder.

"Tell him I want to use the boat," Reid whispered. "I want to do a couples' activity for four hours."

Kathy looked at him with a raised eyebrow, then she covered the phone.

"So, she is not that important, huh?"

Reid waved at her while she was on the phone. There was no doubt that Kathy was going to go ahead and get this set up for him. It's just a funny thing when you're setting up your own execution block. Kathy hadn't met Gloria yet, but she doubted that Gloria would want her to stay around. As she relayed the information to Petr, her heart sank, but her smile never faltered. After Kathy hung up the phone, she turned and looked at her brother.

"You need to be honest with yourself, Big Brother. You are acting like you're trying to keep this woman."

Reid shrugged.

"I don't know what I'm trying to do with her yet, and do I really need to know right now?"

Kathy shrugged. "If you are really going to go all out in order to get this woman, it seems like you would be wanting to impress her from the start."

"It's not that easy, Kathy."

"Reid, this isn't the first time that you've gone out with a woman. What's different now?"

"She says that she's not really interested in a relationship right now."

"And you don't think she's telling the truth?" Kathy looked at her brother skeptically.

"Let's just say that, if she really didn't want me to be there, she could have cut me down in so many other ways. At the very least, I think she's just as curious about me as I am about her."

"Well, for what it's worth, I'm glad that she has enough backbone to stand up to you. You can be a force of nature sometimes. However, all of that being said, just remember, if she comes to the point when you know she doesn't want to be with you, be ready to walk away."

Reid nodded. "She's so independent, Kathy. I offered to pay for everything to get her from one place to the other so she could see the properties, and she said no."

Kathy gave a little laughter and shook her head.

"So, it's true. They say men always want the forbidden fruit. Be careful with her feelings, Reid."

This had to be the hardest thing that Kathy had ever done. Listening to her big brother try to figure out why Gloria didn't want him, and all the while she knew that this was going to push her out of his life. She would never stand in the way of Reid's, happiness.

"I'm not sure where this is going, Kathy, but I just don't want to mess it up."

"Then listen to me, Big Brother. If she is as special as you think she is, what you need to do is to get to know her. The rest of the world has already made assumptions about her because of the way she looks, or she carries herself. Your job is to find out who is the real her underneath there and then cherish it."

"What does that even mean? Why can't you just give me some straight instructions that I could read and do? You know, something like pick up 'A.' Give her object 'B.' Tell her 'Y.'"

"What I'm saying to you is, don't focus on all the external stuff you see about her."

"Okay, so you want me to get to know her true nature, and just how will I know I am looking at her true nature?"

"You know you're at her true nature when you close your eyes, and you see a woman with flaws, and they make her more beautiful."

"And if I can't find it?" Reid said quietly.

"She's not Joyce."

"You're right," Reid said sullenly.

"Besides, she does financial planning. A woman who manages money is pretty no-nonsense, and if you get lost, she probably has a backup plan for you to see the real her."

"A beautiful financial planner," Reid says.

"Trust that you deserve this, Reid. Joyce was a snake lying in the grass. This Gloria sounds better."

"I like her, Kathy."

"You like her, do you? You mean like her, like you want a house, a dog, a cat, and 2.5 kids kind of like her?"

Reid laughed. "I'm drinking the Kool-Aid. that doesn't mean I'll believe everything that's told to me. Strong attraction, yes. Marriage and kids? I'm not sure I'll ever be the one. I'm not ready to be pinned down."

Kathy reached out and touched Reid's shoulder.

"You know, it's possible that commitment doesn't mean a slow death."

"I hear you, Kathy, but I haven't seen it yet. Even if I could find that special person and they made it past the first hurdle of accepting me as I am, the money would complicate things. Nope! It's better to enjoy life and not be tied down."

Kathy didn't argue with him. She heard what he'd said, but she learned a long time ago to look at what people actually do if you want to know what is in their hearts.

"Well, let's not think on such dark thoughts. Let's see if we can find something for you to wear to Montauk tomorrow and look dignified."

Reid looked appalled. "I always look good in my clothes. What are you talking about?

Kathy rolled her eyes. "Yeah, yeah, yeah, mister jeans that leave nothing to the imagination and shirts that are waiting for you to flex just a little bit so you can bust out of them," Kathy said as she left the room. This time, Reid didn't follow, but Kathy heard him sputtering in disbelief.

CHAPTER 6

*G*loria was prepared for Reid today. She had on her black Armani suit. Underneath, she had on a silk chemise. All of that, paired with her favorite black pumps, she was fully armored. With the ensemble she had on, there was no way Reid was going to get past go.

"Gloria, my heart can start beating again. Here is Petr Kozlov and welcome to Heaven's Gate," Reid said.

Gloria gave him a smile. Her armor was starting to crack, and she hadn't even been around him for five minutes.

"Hello, Ms. Danvers, my name is Petr, and I welcome you. How was your travel?" Petr asked as he held out his hands in greeting.

"The travel was great. The drive wasn't as long as I thought it was going to be." Gloria thought she would just have to hold out for a few more minutes. Surely, Reid would leave and then she could start to assess the property without his distracting presence.

"Mr. Kozlov, can we sit as I collect some basic information from you? It will help me with my figures and baselines."

"Only if you call me Petr."

Gloria took out her black portfolio, and then she started to talk about the size of the property, the amenities offered, as well as the employees. When Gloria started to collect the information, she forgot about everything except the answers and that old thrill started to come back. Gloria had always loved numbers. Numbers fit, and they made sense. Her home life wasn't stable, but what was always stable and made sense were numbers. No matter what else was going on, Gloria knew numbers would add up. Numbers would never abandon her. Numbers would never leave her and her brother alone because they were too wrapped up in grief from the loss of a spouse. Numbers were consistent, and they could be counted on. After she realized she had gotten all of the basic data, she looked up and realized that everybody was looking at her. Perhaps, the more important thing was she realized that Reid hadn't left.

"I have to tell you, I have never seen a woman so engaged in numbers," Petr said. "I can't tell you that I have the same love for numbers, but I am very proud of my place so why don't I take you on a tour?"

Gloria would have agreed to just about anything to not be the center of attention. "I'd love to see your place. Not to ruin the tour, but if you could take me to some of the places that seem to be your most profitable, I would really appreciate that."

"Of course."

Petr walked out of the room and out of the corporate offices into a hallway. He turned to the right into an elevator, and from inside the elevator, it looked as if the whole world had changed. While the elevator she came up into the office in was just a plain brown paneled elevator with carpet at the bottom, this elevator was an experience. The panels were pictures of Japanese cherry blossoms around the elevator. The carpet felt lush beneath her pumps. And the buttons didn't even really require you to touch them. They were heat sensitive. There was music pumped into the elevator that was slow, sweet, and instrumental. Gloria glanced around the elevator and saw two little air fresheners in the corner of elevator. She heard the slight hiss and knew they were the source of the floral scent that gently wafted in the air.

Petr guided them to what must be the front desk of the spa.

"Ms. Danvers, I invite you to take a taste of our services. I think it will be the best way to explain what we do well or not."

Gloria looked over at Petr, and she was speechless.

"Petr, you've gone so far by showing me around. You don't have to do this." Gloria tried to reason with Petr, but he wouldn't be dissuaded.

"No this is the least I can do for you and my friend. Enjoy, and I'll be back. If there is something that you feel we missed, please don't be shy in letting me know."

Just when she thought she was going to get rid of Reid, it all went south. Now it seemed as though they were going to be together closer than before. Just when she was trying to formulate a response, Petr was hugging her and speaking to someone else in Russian.

"Now, don't worry about the cost. You want to know why people come, and what makes the most money? I think is the best way."

Petr walked her over to Gloria and looped his arms through hers.

"They will treat you and Reid like family."

As Petr walked away, he threw over his shoulder,

"Reid, tell Kathy thank you for me."

Gloria looked at Reid suspiciously.

"Thank her for what?" Gloria asked.

Reid shrugged. "I told you that Kathy manages the businesses to profitability. Everyone knows Kathy."

"I didn't expect for us to go to a spa. It's not on the schedule, "Gloria said, tapping her book as if it were a shield that would ward off the effects of Reid.

"Ah, yes, all things are planned for you I can't address planning, but what I can say is that sometimes plans, and schedules, don't go as they are written," Reid said.

"I don't think that this is going to be very appropriate."

"We're just having a spa day. I want you to think of me as one of your girlfriends. We just decided to take a break for a couple of hours and see what the spa has to offer."

Gloria looked at him as if he had lost his mind. Looking at him as if he were a girlfriend. She would have to be blind.

"Okay, I'll compromise. We can do one activity, and then after that, we get back to work," Gloria said, trying to remember what services were on the list when she came off the elevator. She'd pick one that would take the least amount of time like eyebrow threading.

"Since everything has already been set up of course, I'll agree, "Reid said.

"Everything's already been set up?"

Reid nodded. "Oh, yes. I knew that he wasn't going to just leave it to someone else to decide. He only wants you to see the best. Reid held out his hand and then looked into Gloria's eyes.

"We will be in a room with a screen between us as we get a deep tissue massage. It's only from the waist down, so don't worry about it. You'll be safely behind the screen, and I will be on the other side."

Gloria was waiting for the trick and trying to find out how this could become any more awkward.

"You said that the owner was someone that you knew. Can't you just make some excuse for us?"

"Would you want to offend him?"

Gloria sighed and gave up. In the grand scheme of things, this really wasn't such a big request. Besides, it wasn't every day that you got a free massage at an up-and-coming spa. It would be perfect if it weren't for the fact that she was thinking more about the person who was going to be on the other side of the screen than the amazing service she was about to get.

"Okay, let's get this done with and move on to the business of the plan."

"That's right, we want to get to the plan as soon as possible," Reid said with a smile. Gloria knew it was harmless, but she wondered what Reid was up to when he made the comment.

~

Gloria should have known nothing was going to go according to plan. A massage that should have taken sixty minutes had taken three hours.

When the both of them were shown to the room, it was just as Petr's brochure had described it. There were heated tables. The massage therapist was at the end of the table, and it was a very nice woman with warm hands. Gloria pulled her pants legs up, determined not to get too comfortable, and the therapist said nothing. Everyone was accommodating to her. She had been completely relaxed until she heard the shuffling on the other side of the screen.

Ten minutes into the massage, he started to talk.

"This calf work is great. Are you getting that deep tissue feel in the middle of your calves?"

Gloria had to admit that the woman's touch was firm, and yes, she was becoming more relaxed with each circle of her thumbs on her calves.

"Yes, I can tell the work lives up to its reputation in the brochures."

Gloria wanted to say that she had experienced enough to know that the quality of the employees was not the issue.

"Just wait until she gets to your feet," Reid said.

Her feet? Gloria pushed herself up and looked at the woman who was at the end of the table. She gave her a smile and then held up ten fingers.

"Ten more minutes, Miss, on your calves, and then I'll get to your feet as well."

Gloria tried to hold her hand up to tell the

woman that she didn't need to have her feet done, but she wouldn't hear it.

"No, no, no, it's fine. Your friend is getting some work done too. We know that you should get the same thing."

Gloria lay back down and tried to control her breathing. Oh, she was going to get the same thing that he was, was she?

"Reid, did you put in an order ahead of time of what you wanted?" Gloria asked, trying to keep her tone light.

"I didn't have to. I usually get the same thing done all the time."

She really wanted to yell out, and just what was that? But she wouldn't disgrace herself in front of all these people, and the room seemed extra quiet.

"Are you okay over there, Gloria?" She could tell from his tone that he knew she wanted to say something, but she wouldn't give him the satisfaction.

"Everything is fine. I wanted to thank you for this moment for me to relax before we do your numbers."

"Numbers? Maybe we should get some lunch, and then we'll talk about those numbers then?" Reid suggested.

"We can get lunch, but we're definitely going to be talking about numbers the whole way. You know, this was a really good idea, after all, to get our minds clear so we can focus on not only the numbers, but I'm sure you'll know about the taxes as well," Gloria said with a smile. If Reid wanted to play, she would play.

"Taxes?"

"Let's not talk about it now. We have all of lunch."

Gloria lay down, and she kept that small victory to herself for the rest of the massage. She just experienced the moment. True to the brochure, it was an experience like she had never had. The ambiance of the room relaxed her, the warm table soothed her, and the therapist knew just when to push and to pull back so that she wasn't in pain. When it was all said and done, Gloria had to admit it she loved it. When she met Reid in the hallway, he looked worried, and she was as relaxed as if she had been doing hours of rejuvenating yoga.

"Don't look so worried, the tax conversation will be light," she said. Gloria could see him take a visible sigh of relief. Then he stopped and looked at her.

"Yes? Is my hair askew?" she asked.

"No, I just realized that this is the most relaxed I've ever heard or seen you," Reid said.

Gloria looked at Reid's face and realized this was the first time she had ever seen him not trying to get her to go do something silly. He just seemed like Reid. Of course, he had already "convinced" her to deviate from her schedule, so he wasn't totally innocent, but this was probably as close as he got. With him smiling, it was hard to hold much against him.

"Well, take a good look. I don't think I do this often."

Gloria waited for him to claim the credit for the moment, but he said nothing. Reid picked up her hand and then kissed it.

"What was the kiss for?"

"Because it's not often that I'm moved, and I didn't want the moment to be forgotten," Reid said.

It was then that Gloria realized that, in this moment, she wanted to entertain the idea of more with Reid. She looked at his brown eyes, looking intently at her. Her gaze fell to his mouth, and she let her mind wonder what it would be like.

Reid cleared his throat. "Be careful, Gloria. I'm only human."

Gloria let out a sigh and turned away from him.

"I said I was human and not crazy." With that, Reid spun her around and pulled her into his arms. He lifted her chin so the both of them were eye to eye. He gave her the chance to turn away. Gloria felt her whole body start to beat in tandem with his. His heartbeat was so strong she could feel it next to hers. All of the warning bells were going off in her head, and she ignored them all. It was just one kiss. As he lowered his head, a slow-burning heat spread throughout her body.

Just before his lips touched hers, he whispered, "I hope you plan on breathing. Otherwise, this is going to be very awkward."

That phrase alone broke the tension between them, and Gloria laughed. Then Reid bent his head the rest of the way, and he kissed her. It was not like any kiss she thought she would be having with Reid. It was almost a chaste kiss and was over before it started, and when it was done, he didn't lift his head away. Instead, he kept himself just a breath above her head.

"This wasn't planned, but it was well worth it," he said.

Just then, they heard the hard footfalls of

someone coming, and they both broke apart like guilty children.

"Reid, are you in there? Why didn't you wait for me? I would have given you a massage."

Reid's hand tightened on hers. Whoever it was must be someone he knew but wasn't fond of. A cold visage came over his face, as the young lady appeared. Gloria thought about the files Petr had given her, and she recalled that this was Delilah, the head of the massage team. The name seemed appropriate. She had been at the spa a while. The trick was to see if Reid would acknowledge her or not.

Reid looked at Delilah and nodded. "Hey, Del. I didn't want to bother you because I knew you were working." Reid said it so indifferently that it was a wonder that the young woman kept a smile on her face.

With her hand on her hip, she leaned against the wall and gave Reid a long look. "You know I always have time for you. How long are you going to be here, and when can we get together?"

Reid shook his head and then pulled Gloria closer to his side. "Really, I don't have any time today or any other time, Del. This is Gloria, and I'm with her now."

"Well, when she goes home, do you want to meet up for dinner?"

"My dinner and my breakfast are both Gloria's."

Gloria felt as though she were in a crossroads. It was true, everything Reid was saying, but the implication was so much more. There was a small part of her that wanted to say, take that Delilah, but she knew it was her pettiness and insecurity that wanted the validation and Reid's attention. Gloria knew wanting Reid's attention was already a sign things had gone too far.

"Oh, is Gloria a friend of Kathy's? Did Kathy come with you as well? You know, it's amazing how talented Kathy is, considering everything she's been through."

Reid placed his arm around Gloria and started walking back to the front desk.

"I'm sorry we don't really have time to stay and chat. Maybe some other time, when I can schedule it, we can actually sit down with one another."

It was as if the woman finally got the hint and took a step back, looking perturbed and frustrated as she watched them walk by.

After they both got themselves together and met at the front desk, Gloria looked at Reid and tried to give him her politest smile.

"I don't think I like the look of this," Reid said.

"There's nothing to like or to dislike."

"I'm sorry about Delilah. There's nothing there. At one time, she really thought that would be, but I tried to dissuade her of that notion right away."

Gloria listened to his excuse, and she accepted it. She wasn't blind. Reid was an attractive man. He had all the hallmarks of what every woman would look for. He was attractive, well-to-do, and funny. She knew right away what she was feeling and whose fault it was.

"Can we just not think about Delilah?" Reid implored her

His boyish grin was in full effect, and Gloria looked at it and held it to her memory.

"I think we're going to just not think about this whole encounter."

She could tell by the way he tightened that he was visibly shocked by her announcement.

"Listen, Reid. I understand that you live a different kind of life with no rules. However, my life has rules. Those rules mean I don't do things without plans, and I think about everything that I do so I don't find myself in uncomfortable positions, like meeting Delilah. I appreciate all that you've done, and I am more than happy to continue helping you out, but I just want to make sure you know this lapse in judgment won't be happening again."

# CHAPTER 7

*H*ow could good plans go up in smoke so quickly? Everything was going beautifully between him and Gloria, and then Delilah showed up.

"She's just one person," Reid tried to explain. He could see that his explanation was falling on deaf ears.

"She's one person that I have to evaluate while I'm looking at your assets."

"Do you want me to send her on vacation while you're here so the two of you don't run into one another?" Reid asked. He wasn't sure how he was going to actually be able to do it, but in order to make things better between him and Gloria, he would give it his best shot.

"No, I don't want you throwing your weight around for me. We don't have that kind of relationship," she grumbled.

Just when he thought things couldn't get any worse, when they finally arrive at the front desk, Petr

SUSAN WARNER

showed up. He was coming up behind Gloria, so she never saw him, and Reid gave a shake of his head, signaling to Petr to turn around and leave.

"I'm sorry. I know this is not what you planned, but I don't think this puts a kink into what you're doing. I—"

"That's the problem here. You don't think? How do you think this is going to be when I'm doing interviews and it gets around that I'm the boss's new girlfriend? It's going to make it twice as hard to find out what things are really there when I talk to people and do the interviews because each one of them is going to think I'm taking tales back to you."

"I don't think that's really fair, Gloria. The people here are pretty faithful to Petr, and he is a hard taskmaster."

He saw her reconsider her statement and then nod begrudgingly.

"You're right. I can see that he puts a lot of effort and work into this spa, and it shows. However, that doesn't take away from what I was saying. I will have to work twice as hard to be taken seriously now that I've been seen with you."

As they walked to the office, he thought about what Gloria had said. She was right. Once again, his actions, no matter how well-meaning they might have been were what caused someone that he might care for to be hurt. He was so lost in his thought that he almost didn't recognize where they were going.

"If you want to go back to the spa room or to the car, you are going in the wrong direction," he said in a low voice.

"Well, I'm not going in the wrong direction because I'm not going to the car right now. I still have to do a final meet-up with Petr. More importantly, I need to explain to him, what has already happened, so he won't hear about it secondhand as well."

Reid was completely lost. "What exactly are you going to go ahead and tell Petr? Nothing happened."

Gloria turned and looked at him and gave him a long searching look before she shook her head and walked the other way.

"Gloria, please talk to me."

She stopped and turned to face him.

"I know you have all of this money and life is very easy for you—or at least it appears to be—but I have to make sure to maintain a professional appearance. No, I completely understand how innocent it was when Delilah saw us, but I want to make sure that Petr understands and that he knows that I'm not just here at your whim."

Reid couldn't have thought of a more farfetched idea than what she was saying. "Gloria, after meeting you, no one would ever think you are anything last than professional and spot-on about what you do. You come with numbers, you're ready to talk about improvement, and you're looking for things to see if they're right, wrong, or indifferent. To get this far with most people, it would have been four meetings and you've already covered it in one."

Gloria gave him a wane smile. "I want to thank you for that. It's important that you recognize that I am a professional regardless of how I acted. Now, I have a job to do because I'm being paid and paid well to do it. So, while the things that you said may seem above and beyond, this is the normal service that my work ethic demands."

"I hope you believe me when I say I would never do anything to make you look less in anyone's eyes. I wasn't trying to ruin your work ethic. I was just trying to have a good time with a beautiful woman, one who looks like she works too much and doesn't enjoy life as much. I may not be good at a lot of things, but I'm usually pretty good at getting people to relax and have a good time."

Reed felt Gloria put her hand on his cheek.

"I don't think that's the only thing that you're good at. I'm just not used to mixing work and any kind of fun. Besides, when I saw Delilah, I thought she might be closer to the kind of woman you really wanted to hang out with."

He shook his head. "It's amazing how astute you are in some areas and in others you just fall right off the cliff. Delilah is a gold digger. I don't know if we're supposed to use the term anymore, but that's what it is. At every opportunity, she has people who let her know when I'm here so she can conveniently rearrange her schedule to be around me."

"That's a lot of work for a woman who's not getting any encouragement," Gloria said.

Reid looked at Gloria and wondered for a moment if her comment came from the possibility that she was jealous. Normally, this would have been one of the times that he would have backed up right away. A woman who was jealous when they hadn't even known each other for a week was a sign that the woman had expectations, and normally Reid didn't do expectations. However, when expectations were coming from Gloria, Reid discovered that maybe it wasn't such a bad thing.

"There's no need for you to be concerned or jealous."

Gloria laughed." Ah, and now the man I know has come back."

Reid smiled. "I never left you, Gloria."

Just then they were interrupted when Petr walked into the room.

"So, you're back so soon after being so relaxed, and what is the verdict?" Petr asked.

Gloria turned and gave Petr one of her famous smiles, and for a moment, Reid was jealous. Then he remembered that Gloria was just taking care of business. He knew the why, but it didn't take away the sting of seeing her so easily smile at another man.

"The spa is run amazingly well. I wanted to let you know about a little run-in I had with an employee named Delilah."

Petr sighed. "If Delilah was involved, it wasn't accidental."

Reid looked at Petr and felt all the worse for him. Gloria looked a bit confused, but Petr was the kind of guy who didn't sugar coat and Reid felt as though Petr was about to deliver some truth that might not bode well for Delilah but might help him.

"I'm sorry, Ms. Danvers. Delilah is my cousin. She's a great masseuse, but she's had a hopeful thing for Reid since she met him that everyone but her seems to know isn't going to work."

He could see Gloria tense up, and while Reid was glad Petr knew the truth, this likely wouldn't help him at all with Gloria.

"Well, thank you, Petr. Why don't I take my

notes, and then we'll set up another time perhaps after this has—"

Petr interrupted her. "You are right. We can reschedule. Why don't we do the morning? There has been a considerable amount of rain and an old tree has taken its last stand over half of the bridge, so traffic has practically crawled trying to get past it."

Gloria looked between Reid and Petr.

"You've got to be kidding, right?" She looked at Reid, hoping he would deny Petr's conclusion. "He's kidding, right, Reid?"

"I'm afraid not. It's one of the not-cool aspects of living up here. It's beautiful all the time and sometimes the place keeps you a day or two. However, I know how you like your schedules, and so I have people monitoring the situation. We will be able to leave in the morning, unless you want to wait in traffic now." Reid was making the offer, but in his heart, he hoped she would stay

"And where would I stay for the night?"

The words brought hope to Reid's soul. "The spa has guest rooms you can stay in for up to a week," Reid offered. "However, I would consider it a privilege if you'd consider staying with me at my place. That way, as soon as everything clears, we can move out right away."

"Your place.?"

"Hold on. Before you start thinking the worst, let me tell you that my place has ten bedrooms, four bathrooms, and two floors. Conceptually, we could be in that house and not even talk to each other or see each other in the run of a day or a night."

Gloria turned around and looked at Petr.

"He's telling you the truth, Miss Danvers. If his

offer is not welcome, my spa is at your disposal. I will be more than happy to share with you until the morning."

Gloria took a deep breath and nodded her head toward Reid.

"I'll stay with you, Reid."

Reid knew this was a big step for Gloria. After everything else that has gone on, he knew she would be justified in being suspicious of him, but the fact that she was willing to give him a chance made him think there was hope for whatever was building between them.

"Let me offer you some more comfort. My sister Kathy came right away when she heard there was a woman here," he said with a smile.

Gloria gave a tremulous smile. "Did she? Will she be the one to tell me the tales of how you have a different guest every week?"

Reid leaned into Gloria to whisper in her ear.

"She knows the truth about me. I'm a private man, and I've never brought a woman home. She's my baby sister. I'm sure it's killing her to know who would make me break one of the few rules I have."

Gloria pulled back. "I'll get our things and meet you outside in the car."

As soon as she walked away, Reid texted Kathy.

*BRINGING A GUEST.*

*IS THIS THE WOMAN?*

*SHE'S THE WOMAN.*

*HURRY UP, I'M EXCITED TO SEE THE WOMAN WHO HAS CAPTURED YOUR HEART.*

Reid wanted to respond that he hadn't said that Gloria had captured his heart. Then he walked out and saw her standing in front of his car and was overcome with a sense of rightness that he wasn't ready to dispute or debate. He could see there were faint worry lines on her face.

"Everything is a go," he said, and then she relaxed. Reid thought it was funny how you could do something for others all the time and it meant nothing. However, when you did an ordinary mundane act and it made someone you cared about happy or relieved their tension, you could feel like a king.

*SHE DOESN'T KNOW SHE'S SPECIAL TO ME.*

*BRING HER, ROMEO. I CAN'T WAIT. STOP WORRYING. YOU ARE THE CAT'S MEOW.*

Reid knew that Kathy loved him above all people. For so long, it had just been the two of them. He hoped she knew that nothing would change between them. As he opened the door for Gloria, his thoughts were brought back to the woman in front of him. If he thought good manners alone would impress Gloria, he would go get decked out in a black suit with white gloves. This was the woman who didn't believe in doing things outside of her schedule, and he was the man who didn't like schedules. However, Reid had to admit that for Gloria, he might be willing to explore a schedule or two.

Then his head reminded him he didn't do relationships and commitment. Reid tried to remember all of the reasons he would never marry or give in to falling in love. Love made people act irrationally. He would help Gloria be the woman he knew was trapped inside and then let her go. She was an amazing woman, and for her to be closed off so early, seemed like a crime. Gloria might be strong enough to endure love without letting it kill her. He knew he would hurt in new ways to see Gloria go off with another man, but it was for the best. He was from bad stock, and he didn't want that to spill over to Gloria. Love never brought anything good to Reid's life.

Just thinking about Gloria with another man was enough to set his teeth on edge. When he got into the car, he had to make sure not to slam the door behind him. He wasn't going to fall into the trap of love. Love wasn't for him. After he settled down in the back seat and the driver began to move, Gloria was quick to ask a question.

"So, Kathy is your sister?"

Reid smiled and nodded.

"She's not just my little sister, she's also my business partner and basically the check and the balance of making sure we make a profit in all of our businesses. She's waiting for us at the house. I think she's going to be really happy for us to be able to have a bite together until the storm passes."

"I hope you didn't tell her to go out of her way for me?"

"No, she'll be happy for the company. I'm afraid being around your older brother isn't the most stimulating thing."

"So, what did you tell her about me?"

"I told her the truth. I told her you were an amazing woman, and I was bringing you home."

Gloria blushed under the compliment.

"What did you think I was going to tell her?"

"I thought you might have told her that you kissed me. I didn't want her to have the idea that there was something going on between us more than there was."

"Oh yes, the kiss. Does that really qualify as a kiss, though?"

"It does. Not that it's ever happening again, but it does."

"What does that mean?"

Gloria smoothed her hands over her pants. "It means that it was unplanned and foolish and caused all sorts of problems, and as a result, it only goes to prove my point. We should never do that or anything unplanned."

Reid smiled. "Ah, so what you mean is we can't do this until you put it on your schedule, and then it's okay for us to do it?"

Gloria looked at him in shock and then started laughing. "Tell me, does that happen to you a lot? When someone tells you they are going to do one thing, and then you use their words to try and get your way? Of course, you add that smile. That is just the icing on the cake."

"I never really looked at it that way. However, I do think it's interesting that you think my smile is the icing on the cake," Reid said.

He was waiting for her rebuttal, when all too soon, they pulled up next to the house.

"What is this?" she said in awe.

Reid looked out the car window and saw the family home and wondered what she was referring to. "Is something wrong?"

"Is this your home, or did you find a hotel, after all?"

"This is the house. I told you I had more than

enough bedrooms and bathrooms, so it's a little bit bigger than most."

They got out of the car, and Reid helped Gloria out of the car. When she took his hand, something clicked in him, and it felt just right. He knew all the excuses he had been telling himself about family and wives were just that, excuses. His heart was gaining ground on his head. Gloria wiped away all of the fears he had been holding on to and gave him a beacon of hope to follow.

"I guess when you say you have a couple of more bathrooms and bedrooms, I wasn't imagining this. This looks like a house you see in the movies where the very rich people live and behind the house, there are horses, land and acreage," she said in awe.

"Well, to answer that question, there are some horses and acreage behind this house. Relative to our neighbors, we have a small plot."

The wind was starting to whip up, and he could feel the first drops of rain beginning to fall.

"Mr. Chance, I'll be leaving now," the driver said as he tilted his head toward Reid.

Before they could even knock on the front door, Kathy whipped open the door to let them in.

"Come in. The rain hasn't started, but I can smell it," Kathy said with a big grin on her face.

"Thank you for inviting me to your home. I really didn't want to impose," Gloria said.

Kathy's smile got wider if that was even possible.

"Please come in. It's nice to have another woman to be able to talk to. My brother loves talking about his adventures, but I've heard them all."

The women went into the house and started talking

as if they were best friends. Reid stood in the doorway and watched them walk off. He had been with Gloria all day long. He had to admit he was a bit jealous of Kathy. Gloria and Kathy were walking hand in hand as if he didn't even exist. Gloria was a complicated woman, but Reid was ready for the challenge.

# CHAPTER 8

*G*oing home with Reid just confirmed all of Gloria's suspicions. What he thought was a home was a palace to her. They were too far apart. It was true that the home had beautiful wooden natural floors. All of the furniture seemed large and comfortable. And while the house was larger than anything that she would have ever thought to buy, it still held an air of family and comfortability to it. The furniture said that this place had been lived in by many a generation and still families could gather here.

"I know you've been with my brother to the spa. Did you need any other clothes? It looks like we might be the same size."

Gloria looked at Kathy and thought they might be the same height, but that was about all. Kathy had beautiful hair, and wide eyes, and she had an open personality that just invited you to talk to her. Kathy had the kind of features every model wanted to have.

"I really don't want to put you out." Gloria hoped that would suffice. Kathy paused for a moment and looked at her.

"Do I sense some hesitation about looking through my closet for some gear?"

"I don't want to be rude, but I'm not really sure we would wear the same size."

Kathy smiled.

"It's not rude. My weight fluctuates, and I never throw out any clothes because I know eventually I'll be back at that size again."

"You never throw anything out, like ever?"

Kathy shook her head.

"Stress tends to be a major factor in my life, and it makes me gain or lose weight. So instead of me buying new clothes all the time, I just keep a range of clothes two sizes up and two sizes down."

Well, there was a lot of logic in that statement, but Gloria had to wonder, why was Kathy so stressed? Was running the business creating all that undue stress in Kathy's life? It seemed odd that Reid would allow her to work at a detriment to herself. It was clear that Reid adored his baby sister. Gloria found their easy camaraderie endearing and showed a different side of Reid that was more attractive than his face. One of the things she appreciated about Reid was his attentiveness. Gloria didn't know the answer, but she would figure it out. When Gloria met Kathy, she felt instant solidarity, and the least she could do was help her out with this.

"Is it running the business that's causing so much stress?" Gloria asked.

Reid came into the living room. Kathy grinned and looked over at her brother. "My stress is my own. Working helps to distract me, most days," Kathy said.

"I completely understand. I find refuge in my work as well."

"Reid is a good guy and allows me a lot of latitude when it comes to my work."

Gloria nodded and then smiled. It wouldn't do to tell Kathy how much of a pain her brother could be. She had rules that Reid didn't like, so he didn't follow them. He wasn't rude or out of line. Reid was just stubborn. Gloria could deal with stubbornness.

"You know, I appreciate your hospitality until the storm passes, but you don't really have to do anything special for me for dinner."

Kathy waved her off.

"I was entirely too nosy to see who my brother would bring home. I was already cooking, so it was no problem to increase the recipe. Reid led me to believe you were a rare woman, one who didn't take his foolishness or fall for his smiles."

Gloria turned to Reid.

"So, I'm a unique woman, huh," she said jokingly.

"I've been saying that all day," Reid said. "Before you two start exchanging stories about me, your bedroom is down the hall, second door on the right."

"Don't be such a pain. Show her the blue room yourself. I thought you were picky, but maybe it's your manners that discourage women."

Reid looked a bit red-faced, but he held his hand to Gloria. "Forgive me, this way."

When Kathy had left, Gloria cleared her throat and tried some conversation. "Your home is beautiful."

"Thank you. It's one of the few places that Kathy and I have as a refuge."

"One of the few places?"

"We have other places we own, but we rent them out for executive long and short stays."

The conversation was stilted as he delivered her to her room. If the overall beauty of the home left Gloria speechless, the room was an ethereal moment. The room looked as though it had come straight out of some romantic story. It had a four-poster bed. It had so many pillows on it, she could probably sink into the pillows alone. The bed was done in white lace and embroidered flowers on the quilt. In front of the bed, there was an ice-pink shag rug. The furniture in the room was made of dark oak. The pieces complimented each other and helped to transport her back to an earlier time.

"It's beautiful," she whispered.

"Yes, you are," Reid confirmed.

Gloria knew she was blushing. Reid held up his hand and backed out of the room.

"I know, I know that wasn't part of the plan and it wasn't on the schedule, but it would be remiss of me not to tell you how beautiful you are."

Just as she was getting ready to respond, they heard the crack of thunder above the home. Gloria shivered and then focused on Reid.

"Thank you for giving me a place. I really should have been looking at the weather front and I didn't see it, but I'm happy that we're not in the storm."

"Emergency planning has always been a strong point of mine, and I'm glad that I could be of service to you. Sweet dreams, Gloria."

Then he was gone. Gloria looked around the

room and took it all in. This was why she was here, to make sure he still had something to pass on to his kids. Whomever the woman was who married Reid, they would be very lucky. She could almost see herself in this setting. What was she thinking? There would be no chance of her ending up with Reid. She wasn't the kind of woman who did forever, and she wanted a calm, regulated, single life.

Gloria shook off those errant thoughts as a result of being surrounded by such opulence. It was a dream come true to be in Reid's house. This was the life of a princess who had nothing to worry about. Gloria took a deep sigh and reminded herself she had real problems that a princess would never have. At the end of the day, it was those problems that had brought her here in the first place. Not wanting to put off the inevitable, Gloria left the room only to find Reid waiting in the hallway for her.

"You didn't have to wait here," she said, a little surprised to see him.

"Did you hear the way Kathy tore into me for not walking you here? There's no way I'm going to walk into the kitchen and not have you on my shoulder."

He extended his arm to her, and for once, Gloria felt like she was committing to more than just an escort.

"I didn't mean to get you in trouble," Gloria said.

Reid snorted. "She's my sister. She'd find any excuse in the book to be able to rag me. It's not you, and she's not serious. Well, she is serious about me being polite to a woman, but she's just playing. There's no problem."

Gloria walked into the kitchen. If she thought the house was large, then the kitchen was made as if someone was going to feed an army. It was filled with stainless steel appliances Everything in the kitchen appeared to be brand new. The countertops were gray and white. If Gloria wasn't mistaken, they were all marble

All in all, it was an impressive sight to see, and only one thing rivaled it: the dining room area. The dining table was made of glass, and there were three settings. In the middle of the table, there were three trays: one tray with bread, one tray with meat, and the last one with vegetables. The layout and the spread of the meal looked like a Rockwell photo.

"Oh, my goodness," Gloria said. Then as if waiting for her cue, Kathy popped out in a dark blue dress.

"Voila! Do you like it?" Kathy asked.

"It looks totally amazing, and I want to thank you for inviting me in."

Gloria tried to take it all in and knew this was not the life that she could possibly live. Gloria must have been standing for too long because Reid tapped her on the shoulder. He walked her to the table and then pulled out the chair for her.

"I want you to know that I asked Reid, and he said you had no food allergies. Was that correct?"

"Yes, it's true."

"Well then, this is going to be an easy meal. Bon appétit."

The meal was amazing and occurred with no issues. In fact, Gloria was so thrilled that she agreed to come back when Kathy said they had to do dinner again. For once, Gloria felt as though she had a real friend in Kathy.

After dinner was done, Kathy wanted to know everything about Gloria.

"So, explain to me exactly what it is that you're supposed to be doing, Gloria," Kathy asked.

"Oh, I hope you don't feel offended or mind my being here. Grayson sent me here just to review all of Reid's latest holdings and to make sure that he has a way to manage them. I'm sure I mentioned before that Grayson is getting married and wants to make sure all of Reid's affairs are correct since he won't have time to be looking at them."

"I never thought that any of the Chance men would ever bite the bullet and settle down," Kathy murmured.

"If you saw Grayson, you would see how utterly happy he is. It's no surprise they are engaged and looking at planning their marriage," Gloria said.

Reid chimed in, "He's so happy that he forbade Vincent to look her up."

"No way!" Kathy said. "Wow, that is really serious."

Gloria looked between them, and then Kathy looked at her and practically jumped up.

"I'm so sorry, Gloria. We should have explained. Vincent is the suspicious brother, if ever there was one. He has everyone researched and swears that he will never be able to find a woman who will be able to survive his background check. If Grayson told Vincent not to do a background check, this is the ultimate form of trust. That, of course, will rub Vincent the wrong way because he cares about Grayson."

Gloria was shocked. "He investigates the women he dates?"

Reid held up his hand. "Well, that's not the only ones he investigates. He investigates potential spouses and business associates as well."

Kathy waved away her brother's answer. "I haven't heard the whole story, Gloria, but Vincent's paranoia seems like it came as the result of a woman. Vincent's loss made him become a worrier determined to protect his brothers from the same treacherous fate."

"He's dealing with it the best way he can, Kathy," Reid said in defense of Vincent.

Gloria looked at both of them at the table. This discussion was an old argument. Outside, Gloria could hear the roll of thunder as it approached.

During the time she had been listening to the thunder, Kathy had gotten up from the table and brought back a tray with coffee and tea.

"So, I hear that you are very good at doing financials, but you didn't want to help me with mine," Reid said to Gloria.

Kathy laughed. "Ignore him, Gloria. He's just put out that you didn't want to help him."

"It wasn't personal. I think that finance is a personal issue. I used to do financing, and I chose to walk away," Gloria said.

"So, are you taking a hiatus?" Kathy asked.

Gloria looked at the inquisitive looks from the both of them and knew this wasn't going to end unless she was rude or if she just answered the question they were trying to get to.

"I am very good at finances, and at one time, I

made a significant amount of money doing so," Gloria said.

Kathy reached out her hand and touched Gloria. "So, what happened?"

Gloria straightened her back and then cleared her throat. She could do this. "When I was working in finance, I became pregnant. I would work eighteen to twenty hours a day, and eventually, it took its toll on me. I had already been pushing myself to exhaustion and being pregnant wasn't any help. I wouldn't listen to anyone, thinking that it would somehow be okay. I thought I was built to do everything all at once. I lost the baby. From that point on, I really couldn't keep working in finance without having the memory come up. So, that's my story."

There was silence in the room, and this was the part that Gloria hated the most. She never wanted to be the center of attention, and she also didn't want to have anyone pity her.

"Well, this makes all the sense why you didn't want to have anything to do with finance now," Reid said.

"Let's just say that if I wasn't in dire straits, I wouldn't have even considered a finance job."

Gloria looked over at Kathy, and she looked totally confused.

"Go ahead, Kathy. We've gone this far. What else did you need me to answer?"

"Well, you said you were really successful at it. I'm not quite sure what conditions pushed you to come back into it."

Gloria looked at Kathy, and she could tell that

her tenaciousness was one of the things that she and her brother shared.

"He would be right to say that I have a lot of investments, but a majority of those are in things I can't easily take out without a heavy tax penalty. I was in a relationship with another very successful finance person, and we had everything in joint accounts. Needless to say, that when I got ready to leave, his vision was different from mine. He thought I just needed time to recoup and regroup."

"Gloria, I'm so sorry. We were so inconsiderate to make you relive that," Reid said.

"You know, at first, I thought it was pushy of you to keep asking me, but now I realize to heal, I can't hide from it. Talking about it clears it from me." The silence was oppressive. "I want to thank you for an amazing dinner and for letting me stay the night," Gloria said.

"It's my pleasure," Kathy said.

"Do you need help to—" Reid said

Gloria met Reid's gaze and smiled. "I'm fine. I can find the bedroom, and I'll see you both in the morning."

# CHAPTER 9

$\mathcal{T}$he information from last night still stuck with Reid.

Once again, in his arrogance, Reid had trampled over Gloria's privacy, thinking he could help. While it was true Kathy had done most of the talking, Reid could have stopped her at any time, and he hadn't. He could just bang his head over how he had been as delicate as a sledgehammer.

Last night, he had seen a new part of Gloria, and he hadn't been prepared. How arrogant of him to think he could help her overcome such a loss. He thought he would find the kitchen empty in the early morning. What he found instead was Gloria working on the kitchen table.

"Oh, you're up. I'm glad because I wanted to get started on the write up. I didn't think you would wake up until much later. I'm starting to put together some simulations of your finances, and I thought it would be a good time for us to go over it."

"I need to talk to you."

"Well, that doesn't sound like a conversation I want to have," Gloria said.

He walked around the table and took the seat nearest to Gloria. Gloria scooted back a little bit and looked at him oddly.

"Reid, what's wrong?"

"You confuse me."

"Uh huh? I hope you don't think that's a fully qualified answer."

"Yesterday, I was wrong. I pushed you beyond your limits. I got you to expose something about yourself that really should have been your choice about when you told me. I was selfish. I'm sorry, and I didn't mean to bring up something that was extremely painful for you."

"Reid. It's fine. It's over. Let's not talk about it."

"I think we do need to talk about it because I'm not one to do something and then run away from it."

"It's not wrong to want to know about another person."

"It's wrong to push a person that you care about."

"Reid, you shouldn't care about me. After hearing my story last night, I would think that it would be even clearer to you while there couldn't be anything between us. I'm still putting the pieces of my life together."

"I don't know that I believe that. I think that you have all of your pieces together, but you're scared.

Gloria gave him a sad smile. "You are forever looking for that spin and angle, Reid. I am not as brave as you may think. I'm just a regular woman trying to live day by day. I'm a bad risk."

Reid reached out and pulled her hands into his.

"I think that if you see someone worth taking the risk on, you should go that extra mile for them."

"So, do you see someone worth going that extra mile for? Do you think you're the man for this job?" she asked.

"I'm hoping that it's someone like me. To be honest, I'm hoping it is me. You are a wonderful and amazing woman, and you have so much to give."

"Giving comes at a cost," Gloria said.

"You're right, it does. We all need to make the decision of when we feel it's time to take a chance. More importantly, we need to decide who we want to take the chance with."

Gloria stood up and reached her hand out to cradle his cheek.

"If ever I was going to take a chance, you would definitely be my first pick, Reid. I don't think that I'm ready for a relationship. There's too much of me that's still broken, but I'd appreciate it if we could be friends."

A little part of Reid curled in on itself. Friends. It wasn't what he wanted but this was about Gloria. If it turned out that's all they could be, he would bury his feelings and do this for her. When Reid looked at Gloria, he saw a butterfly that had recessed back into its cocoon, too afraid to fly. A butterfly who didn't realize that staying in the cocoon was dooming it to never fly again.

Just like that, Kathy came into the kitchen, and their moment was gone.

"Wow, you two are up early. Reid is usually just going to bed when the sun is rising." Reid looked at Kathy, and although all of the right words are coming out of her mouth, something was wrong. He could see that she seemed a little off. When he tried to catch her attention, she avoided his gaze. Reid shook his head and wondered what made him think he ever knew anything about women. Just when he was about to reach out to Kathy and ask her to meet him in the other room, his phone rang.

"Good morning, this is Reid. Petr, just what I need in my life right now."

"Hey, is that Petr on the phone?" Gloria asked.

Reid groaned inwardly. He had just been regulated to a friend, and Kathy was less than happy with him, but he had no idea why. To top it all off, Gloria seemed way happier to talk to Petr than share time with him. He was just on a losing streak with all the women in his life.

"If Gloria has any questions, I'll answer them now if you want, unless you want me to come over for breakfast and stay for the day," Petr teased Reid on the phone.

Reid was in no mood to deal with Petr's sarcasm.

"You can speak to her now, and no, I don't expect to see your mug anytime in the next seventy-two hours."

Reid handed the phone to Gloria, who looked at him with a smile and then shook her head. After a few moments, Gloria was off the phone and looking very relieved and proud of herself.

"I take it all went well," Reid said.

"It did. Everything else I can actually do from home now that the storm is done. If I hurry, I'll be able to get home in time."

"In time?"

"Yes, tomorrow is going to be the equinox, and I would like to be home," she said with a quiet smile.

To say that Reid was curious would have been an understatement.

"If you want, we can do something here for the equinox." Reid was at a loss. He didn't know what was so special about the equinox, but he was willing to learn something new with Gloria.

Reid saw Gloria hesitate, and then after a few moments, she let out a small sigh.

"I have standing dinner plans on the equinox, so I would prefer to be able to get home. The storm has passed. Is this going to be an issue? I can get myself back to the bay."

Reid held up his hand. It galled him that she wanted to leave him to run to another man after she had just finished saying that he could only be friends.

"I plan on going into the city tomorrow. Why don't you just stay with us for another day?" Kathy asked.

"I really do need to make it home today," Gloria pressed.

"It's no problem, really." Reid said the words, but they were the furthest from his heart. "I'll be more than happy to get you back home today. I'll call the driver, and we can leave in an hour. I wouldn't want to keep your gentleman waiting."

"And how are you so sure it's a guy?" Gloria asked

"I've found that most of the time when women won't break a date or move an arranged meeting, it's usually because there's a man involved. I could be wrong. Am I?"

He watched Gloria blush, and she shook her head. Then Kathy came farther into the kitchen and took a seat next to Gloria.

"Well, I have to admit, I'm kind of intrigued. And if my brother won't ask, I will. Who's the hot guy?"

Gloria looked at her for a moment and then started to laugh. Reid and Kathy looked at one another waiting for her to explain the joke.

"It's not as clandestine as the two of you would make it seem. Today is the day that my father passed away at sea, and I usually go out to dinner on this day. My father loved the sea, worked at sea, and he died at sea. It's tradition for Jack and me to go to dinner to commemorate that passing."

Jack. What kind of name was Jack? Just when it seemed like she was going to say something more, her phone rang. Reid wanted to stand right there until her phone call was done and then continue to ask her about Jack. But then memories of yesterday came back to him. He wouldn't make the same mistake twice. Intruding in her life where she hadn't invited him.

He would take her back to Inheritance Bay, and he wouldn't say a thing about whomever this Jack was.

# CHAPTER 10

"I hope we can be friends, no matter what happens with you and Reid," Kathy whispered to Gloria. Kathy whispered her request in Gloria's ear as they said their goodbyes. When Gloria pulled back, she could see the sheen of tears in Kathy's eyes.

Her intent had been to come and review an investment, and now she was leaving with a friend and the sense of having found a little more of herself. Gloria knew that she was able to face her past. She wasn't sure that she was ready for Reid, but she was sure that she was stronger than she thought she was.

Kathy had given her some seeds and a plant. Gloria had tried to explain she was talented in killing things, even seeds that hadn't made it into the ground yet.

"If something should happen to them, it will give you an excuse to come and see me sooner."

"If I came back every time something died, I'd

have to move in with you," Gloria says. "It would be cheaper to keep me with you."

Kathy blinked her eyes very quickly and then pulled Gloria into her embrace.

"You are priceless to Reid and to me," she says. "And I know this may sound odd to you now, but if Reid doesn't keep you, I will."

Gloria gave a sad sigh. "I don't think I'm a keeper yet, but I'm working on it."

"If he can't recognize how rare you are now, he doesn't deserve you. I don't care if he is my brother."

Gloria realized they could go on forever, and the conversation was becoming more and more sentimental.

"Remember, Kathy, you are one of a kind too. This thing clicks with us because the both of us are totally amazing."

Kathy stood back and gave Gloria a look of disbelief. "If you say so. Don't forget to come back and visit."

"I'll make sure to keep everyone updated on all of the business," Gloria promised.

Before they could launch into another conversation, Reid cleared his throat. "Your carriage awaits, my lady," Reid said with a low bow.

Gloria got into the car, and there was a little tinge of sadness that the new friend and the gallant Reid followed. The drive to Inheritance Bay was quiet, to say the least. After ten minutes of quiet with empty flatlands going by, Gloria started to fidget, wondering how long it would be before she was back home.

Then Reid's phone went off, and it was like a collective sigh happened and the silence was broken.

"Reid here." He said very little while on the call, but Gloria could see from his face that Reid was not happy with whatever was being said to him. "Are we sure that there are no other causes for this?" Reid leaned his head back as if the weight of the world was on it. Whoever was on the call were not friends of Reid's. When Reid hung up the phone, it looked like he had given away all of his energy. Curiosity was eating at Gloria, but she waited. In finance and in yoga, holding still could be a lifesaving exercise.

Reid started to fidget until he was patting down his pants. Finally, he found what he was looking for, a stick of gum. After a couple of chews, he closed his eyes. "That was the security man who works in the greenhouse with Kathy."

"You have a security person in the house with Kathy? Is something wrong, or have you decided that your brother Vincent is right and that no one can be trusted?" Gloria asked, trying to add some levity to the situation.

"I have a security person with Kathy because she's an attractive woman, and she wouldn't take a guard on the grounds. The other reason I have him is because every so often, my sister decides that my life would be so much better without her in it."

"What?"

Reid looked at Gloria who was staring at him in shock.

"You mean she tries to hurt herself?" Gloria asked in disbelief.

Reid shook his head. "No, she doesn't try to hurt herself. She tries to pack a bag and then go on a trip. A trip I might add that she has no intention of ever coming back from."

Gloria looked at Reid, but she knew her face must have been a mask of utter confusion. "Come again?"

"When big changes happen in my life, Kathy tends to think that she doesn't want to add to my problems. At first, she just moved to another house and said she needed some space, but then I went to check on her one day and found her leaving with all of her clothes in suitcases. It was then that she explained to me that she didn't want to be a burden to anyone. She was going to leave me for my own good."

Gloria was shocked at first but then when she thought about Kathy, it all made sense. Now the issue about her clothes and her having so many clothes with so many sizes made sense.

"She loves you an awful lot."

Reid grunted. "That's the problem. Love doesn't seem to be invigorating for our family."

"You can't mean that."

He opened his eyes and let out a big breath.

"You've shared so much these last couple of days. Let me do the same. When it comes to love, I know that it always ends in heartache. My mother loved someone, and she wound up leaving her kids for love. Kathy loves me and wants to make sure I'm okay, that I'm not suffering. So, she was thinking about leaving me for love. Every time someone does something that will inevitably hurt someone else, you can usually find love somewhere around. My brother Grayson found Rose, and maybe they will prove me wrong, but as far as I can tell, love always leads to pain."

Gloria was at first shocked and then sad. She

reached her hand out, and Reid covered hers with his.

"Love is the only thing that makes life worth living. Even though I went through loss, I can tell you that there was nothing like the love I felt during that time in my life. You aren't doing yourself or Kathy any good by hiding away from love. In fact, you'll realize that if you try to protect yourself by not admitting you want to have love in your life, you'll live from one moment to another moment, but you won't have meaning in your life."

Reid looked at Gloria as if she had spoken in a foreign tongue.

"You think it's all worth it?"

Gloria nodded. "Even with the pain, I think everyone is supposed to love. It's not just for a few. It's for us all. Besides, think about what would have happened if you hadn't loved Kathy enough to search for her."

He nodded and then looked out to the side window.

"I know. She wasn't in a good place when I found her. I am grateful every day that I was able to get her. I can't make up for the times that I wasn't there, but I try to make sure that she has everything that she needs now."

Gloria's heart was breaking for this man who loved so much but didn't know it. She saw Reid and saw the man who couldn't have been more loving if he tried.

"It's not your job to fix Kathy," Gloria whispered.

Reid turned to Gloria, and she was shocked to see an errant tear running down his face.

"You don't understand. I have to make sure that Kathy is okay because it's my fault that we were separated."

Gloria stilled and waited. There had to be more to this story than the confession that Reid had just given.

"When I was a kid, I was so angry when Kathy came along. I would have to watch her all the time. It was a big hassle because my mom was always moving, and I'd have to share and do things with Kathy. She was so small with little legs, and I was angry having to take care of her."

"Did you take her to the foster care home?"

Reid shook his head. "No, I didn't."

"Did you sign her away to the home or find a nearby social worker and give Kathy to them?"

"No, I didn't do any of those things, but I did tell my mom that I didn't want her. Then one day, I told my mom that we could move faster if we didn't have her with us."

"Then I woke up one morning, and she was gone. My mom told me that she had been listening to me and had taken her to someone who wanted to care for a little girl."

Reid leaned back against the seat and closed his eyes. Gloria couldn't do anything but hold on to his hand. She closed her eyes and tried to understand the guilt Reid had been going around with all of his life. Looking at the scenery go by, so many things made sense.

"Have you spoken this thought to anyone?" Gloria asked.

"I've told my brothers," he whispered haggardly.

"Do they think you are to blame for her being taken away?"

"No, they tell me all the time that I was just a child."

"You don't believe them?"

Reid's voice dropped an octave lower.

"I think that sometimes children can do things and not understand the consequences. It doesn't make the results any less real. For a long time, I searched for Kathy. I was determined to do right by her. I told her when I found her that I was sorry and that I was to blame for the life she had lived.

No one can go back and undo time or experiences, but I can make sure she has everything a woman can want.

"Reid, you can't hold on to this and keep her in a glass bowl. She has to be free to enjoy her life and know that no matter what, you will be here for her. You are giving her the means to not have to take risks and live. The money may give her anything she wants, but the way the two of you are using the money—it's becoming a type of prison."

"It seems like we all have that in common, Gloria. One way or another, we are all hiding from something."

Gloria pulled her hands back and turned to look out the other window. There wasn't anything to say because it was too close to the truth. Reid didn't try to say anything, and the rest of the trip was held in silence. As the car arrived in Inheritance Bay, Reid broke the silence.

"It's late breakfast or early lunch. I know you have a dinner date; would you like to have a quick lunch with me?"

Gloria looked at him and wondered what he was about, but she nodded. The car pulled up to a small starter home. It was such a contrast to his home they stayed in last night. The driver brought in the luggage and even he had to take a second look around the home.

"Mr. Chance, do you want me to take your luggage to a hotel or—"

Reid laughed. "I'm staying here, and I'll be okay. I'll call if I need to go anywhere."

With a nod, the driver was gone, and Gloria looked at Reid.

"I have to say, when you said lunch, I wasn't sure what we were eating, and I'm still not sure," she said with a smile.

Reid walked over to the small kitchen and opened up the refrigerator.

"This is a place that I got for myself to stay at. I haven't been here but a handful of times, but I figured I needed a place to stay so I wasn't in the way of Grayson, Rose, and the twins."

Gloria took another look around the room and could see little touches of Reid. A trophy in one place, a picture of Kathy in another. It wasn't settled in, but she could see him trying to make the space his. The fact that he thought he needed another place to go was a whole other discussion.

"I'm going to make some peanut butter and jelly sandwiches; would you like some? It's only the best grapes that have been used to make this jelly," Reid said in a fake Parisian accent.

Gloria couldn't help but laugh.

"I don't know, I'm used to the leftover grapes. The sandwich may be too rich for my blood."

Reid pulled out some bread from the refrigerator.

"Ah, mademoiselle, do not despair. We have this very common bread. The bread will dilute the specialness of the grapes and make this sandwich good for all people to eat."

"Fine, but I want it to go on record you forced me to do it. If it turns out that I turn into a princess, it will be all your fault!" Gloria said jokingly.

Reid gestured for her to take a seat at a small table that at best could seat two.

"I'd like to talk over lunch," Reid said.

"Okay," Gloria said hesitantly. "It sounds like the sandwich is the bait to get some poor person here, and I am today's victim."

As Reid prepared the sandwiches, he wiggled his eyebrows and then looked at Gloria as if she were the lunch instead of the sandwich.

"I wasn't going to ask anything, but since you brought it up, I would love to ask you a question and then I'll ask you one."

"Fine, what do you want from me, Reid?" Gloria asked. "You have almost everything, and if you don't, I'm sure you are working on it."

Reid finished his sandwiches and then put them on a plate and cut them into triangles.

"I have to tell you, Gloria, you are a hard woman to get to know. However, let me say, as your male friend and all because we established that you aren't ready for anything else, to date, it has been worth the adventure."

"Yes," Gloria said, hoping to move Reid along.

"I'm beyond curious about who Jack is. I mean, I know that you had friends before you met me, but you seem so determined to get back to see this Jack. I mean, his name is Jack for goodness' sake," Reid grumbled as he took a bite out of a triangle.

~

Two weeks of school had gone by, and Hanna wasn't happy.

It was time to read, and Grayson was with Anna. It seemed like everybody liked Anna because she could remember a lot of book stuff. Hanna got up and went into the living room and saw Grayson and Anna clearing up the toys. Who liked to clear up toys?

"Hey, Hanna, you want to help?"

"No, I want to read now," she said.

Grayson stood up and sighed. "We are going to read, but we need to clean up first. We don't want Mommy to come home to a messy house, do we?"

Hanna had to think long and hard.

"I don't know," Hanna said.

Grayson stopped, and he looked confused.

Anna started laughing. "You know Mommy said he's still in training. He doesn't do 'I don't knows' really good yet."

Hanna wanted to laugh with Anna, and she started to, but then she remembered the problem. Everybody laughed with Anna. Anna like to clean the rooms and do her homework and be at the first of the line. No one laughed with her anymore, not even Anna.

"It's not funny, Anna. Remember, we don't laugh at people. You would remember if we were together in school."

With that, Hanna turned away from them both and went to her room. She wasn't going to cry. She could feel the hot tears coming down, but she wasn't going to cry. She just needed to wait for her mom to come home, and it would be all right. It just had to be.

# CHAPTER 11

*R*eid looked at the expression on Gloria's face and he could tell that this was a surprise question. This Jack fellow was under his skin, and he wasn't sure he could let it go. Her mouth opened and then closed again like a fish out of water.

"Jack is my closest friend."

Reid felt like someone has just gut-punched him.

"You're closest friend? That is high praise coming from you."

Gloria nodded and then took one of the triangles. "I'm a lot like Kathy, Reid. I don't do friends, and when I do make them, I tend to keep them. Jack is special. He's funny and he's reliable."

Reid heard her describing Jack, and he sounded like a bad video you would watch on television. Why would she want to be with someone like that?

"So, it's someone old, fat and safe, your saying?" Reid suggested.

Gloria laughed. "I would never describe him that

way. If I even told him he was heading that way, he would probably start hitting the gym even more than what he does now."

"Oh, so he's like a gym rat that doesn't have a job but looks good walking around the sweaty, nasty gyms?"

Gloria shook her head again. "Actually, he's a business owner. He opened the latest Claws place in the park. He used to work as a chef and then decided that he would open his own place. He had a restaurant for a while, but he got tired of that and came to Inheritance Bay."

"So, he's a food truck kind of guy?" Reid said with a smile. He was enjoying playing this game with Gloria.

"I will tell you that he is his own type of guy, and I'm surprised that you don't know him. In small towns, it seems like news of people travels quickly."

Reid considered her words and nodded.

"Normally, you would be right, but I don't spend a lot of time here and when I do, I am in and out so quickly there is no time to be brought up to speed."

"Well, Jack is a bedrock and foundation in my life."

"Okay, so where is this bedrock going to take you for dinner?"

"We are going to a restaurant called the Brine and Salt."

"Brine and Salt? Isn't that a chain restaurant?" Reid asked. "He owns his own business, and you two are going to the Brine and Salt?"

"What is wrong with Brine and Salt? I love their broils that they serve in a plastic bag. I mean, it's amazing how they just put it all into one bag and let it simmer."

"Oh, so the reason you are going is because you like to go?" Reid asked as he popped another triangle into his mouth. "Who's paying for the meal? I know how tough things can be when you first open a business."

Gloria laughed.

"He can afford to go to some other place, but it has been a tradition that we always go to Brine and Salt. Besides, we can sit at the table for hours, and no one bothers us. It allows us to catch up on old times."

Reid couldn't believe he was being beat out by a man who wouldn't even take her to a real fine dining establishment.

"The sandwiches are almost done, and you know what I really want to know? Are you and Jack a thing?" Reid felt like he was at the top of a mountain that he'd never skied before that was treacherous but laid with fresh snow. There was no feeling like it in the world, but the anxiety before you went down could cripple a person. It was that exhilarating but crippling feeling that he had now as he waited for Gloria to answer.

"Jack and I aren't a thing, and if you understood our relationship, you would understand how ewww that really is. Jack is there to do just what I said. He's there to hold my hand and help me remember the good out of times that weren't always good."

"How long have you two been doing this meet up?" Reid questioned.

Gloria stopped and gave Reid a long look. "It's been a long time. Why?"

"I'm just suggesting that the two of you don't have the same end goals."

"What does that mean?" Gloria asked.

Reid sat back in his chair and crossed his arms.

"I am saying if you two have been doing this for a while, then he's just living in the past and he's doing it with you."

Gloria looked at him and shook her head. "Jack doesn't want to live in the past. What you're saying doesn't make any sense."

"Really? I think it's pretty clear. I know you are aware enough as a woman to know when a man is romantically interested in you. So, I'm going to say he's not in love with you. Then we have to look at what other reason could he be doing this ritual for. The other reason a man would do this ritual is because it's a great moment in their life to relive."

"How can you come up with such drivel when you've never even met him? He's in the same town you visit, and you more than likely have eaten from his place in the park, and you can't remember. However, you supposedly know him well enough to make sweeping assumptions about him?"

"You are right. I can't recall if I've ever seen him or not, but what I do know is how a man's mind works. When men are around amazing women, they want to be needed. You are so giving, Gloria, that they have to feel worthy of that love."

"I've known Jack all of my life. He knows he's worthy of my love. He doesn't need to earn it."

"If you've known him all of your life, then I want to be the one to say that he definitely wants to be the one whom you can turn to. At least I understand how that relationship is. More importantly, I understand how you see this relationship. Look, all of the triangles are gone."

Gloria looked at the plate and then back at him.

"Where did they go?"

"Ah, you doubted my specialty. My peanut butter and jelly sandwiches have been around the world. I am known all around for them. I am insulted and disappointed that you doubted you would eat them up like children during recess," Reid said with a fake Parisian accent.

"I'm sorry," Gloria said through her laughter.

"Ah, I will be willing to overlook this major blow to my ego and my reputation that is known all throughout the world."

"Oh, will you?" Gloria prodded. "Tell me, great one, what will get you to recover from this slight?"

"I would like the last of the jelly?" Reid said. He watched Gloria look at the plate and then back at him.

"I'm sorry I ate the last sandwich, and there is none left," she said smiling.

Reid reached out and traced her ear. Gloria's smile faltered and then she moved closer to Reid. They were both leaning on the little table when his finger traced her jawline and then lifted her head up so he could look into her face.

"Yes, this is the face I'd want to be a hero to. Let's go out tonight, and I will fly us to Paris so you can see where the grapes we ate today came from," Reid said as he got within a hair's breadth of her lips.

"I can't stand Jack up. At this rate, you may be too full of yourself for me to see again, outside of me finishing up your portfolio evaluation."

Reid heard the words and remembered his conversation with Kathy. At the end of the day, he would let Gloria lead the way. Instead of finishing the kiss that Gloria was offering, he pulled himself back and sat in his chair.

"Let it be known that your wish is my command." He didn't know where he found the strength to do it, but he sat back and then talked of nothing but his portfolio. He could see Gloria stutter for a moment, but then she picked up the topic and the rest of the afternoon was him talking about numbers while he was trying to get through a meal with a woman he was pretty sure, despite all attempts, he had fallen in love with.

*IT'S OVER!*

Kathy saw the words on her phone and wanted to scream. How could it be? She was so sure that the both of them would be able to make a go of it.

*WHAT HAPPENED?*

*NOTHING HAPPENED. I DID WHAT SHE WANTED. SHE WANTED TO JUST TALK ABOUT MY PORTFOLIO, SO I GAVE IT TO HER.*

Kathy sat down on her bed and dropped her head into her hands. How could it be that her brother who could make grown men tremble, and cry was having a problem with this woman?

*DID SHE TELL YOU TO GO AWAY?*

*CLOSE ENOUGH.*

Again, Kathy wished she was sitting in front of her lug head brother, instead of trying to troubleshoot via text. Reid didn't realize how precious what he had was. He came and found her so she could live a life worth living. She would do her best to make sure she helped him to live the best life, and to her, that meant he needed to find a person to love.

*THERE IS NO SUCH THING.*

*SHE SAID SHE SHOULDN'T SEE ME OUTSIDE OF WORK.*

*AND.......*

*AND WHAT? SHE DUMPED ME.*

Egos, that was what Kathy was dealing with here.

*YOU KNEW SHE WASN'T GOING TO BEND TO YOUR WILL.*

*THERE IS NO BENDING HERE. SHE JUST THREW ME AWAY AND KEPT ON GOING. THE REST OF THE NIGHT WE TALKED ABOUT MY INVESTMENTS.*

*SO, TELL ME, IF YOU DIDN'T WANT TO MARRY, WHY ARE YOU UPSET NOW?*

*BECAUSE I'M AN IDIOT. BECAUSE I CAUGHT FEELINGS FOR HER, AND SHE DIDN'T FEEL THE SAME FOR ME.*

*OR MAYBE SHE JUST DIDN'T TELL YOU.*

*WHY WOULDN'T SHE TELL ME?*

*OH, MY DEAR BROTHER, WELCOME TO THE WORLD OF DATING AND LOVE. IT'S WHERE PEOPLE DON'T WANT TO GET HURT BUT THEY WANT THE REWARD OF FINDING LOVE. LET ME KNOW HOW IT GOES.*

Kathy closed her phone and went back to her garden. Reid always did things the hard way, but he did learn, and he always got the goal. There was still a chance for him and Gloria.

# CHAPTER 12

*K*athy was wrong.

He was not looking for love, and he wasn't a part of that sad lot that was moping around waiting to be acknowledged. No, Reid was going to be a part of the aggressive party. In an attempt to distract himself, he tried to call Grayson to go out to dinner with him.

"I'm sorry, Reid. If you had told me earlier, I would have made other arrangements for the twins. We are camping out today to catch up on some family events the twins think they are missing."

Reid heard Grayson's words, but the joy in his voice said that the events with the twins wouldn't be as big of a burden as he made it sound. Then he told him to call Vincent. He and Vincent were having a meeting tomorrow over one of the fundraising events, but Vincent had arrived in the bay.

*VINCENT, ARE YOU UP FOR BUYING ME DINNER?*

Reid wasn't sure if Vincent was up or not, but he would give it a shot.

*OF COURSE, I'LL PAY TODAY SO YOU CAN GIVE ME BACK THE MONEY AT 150% INTEREST.*

*I WANT DINNER. NOT TO BE SHAKEN DOWN BY MY BROTHER.*

*NO PROBLEM. WHERE DO YOU WANT TO GO?*

*HOW ABOUT I JUST SEND YOU AN ADDRESS, AND WE CAN MEET THERE IN ABOUT THREE HOURS?*

*FINE. I LOVE LOCAL SPOTS.*

Reid now had a wingman and time to contemplate what he was about to do. He wasn't going to do anything. He just wanted to make sure she was all right. It wasn't creepy if he was actually getting dinner at the place. He didn't send the address until the very last minute. When he did and Vincent tried to contact him, Reid knew that the best thing he could do was just show up at the Salt and Brine and make the best of it.

Reid has been thinking about what he could say to Vincent over dinner, and nothing came to mind. When Reid got to the hostess she was in her lower twenties, and this job was not her career.

"I'm Reid, a party of two."

"You say you are here for the children's party. It's in the back and—"

"No, I'm not. I'm meeting someone," he said, and the young lady showed him to the bar which was where Vincent found him nursing an orange juice.

"I am hoping you can explain to me why we are at the Salt and Brine. I had to look at the address twice. I wasn't sure if this was a practical joke or not."

Reid just snorted at Vincent and handed him a menu. "Doing new things will help you expand your horizons."

"The last time you were interested in my horizons was when you thought you would look smarter in front of Cora Franks in sixth grade," Vincent replied.

Reid had forgotten, but as usual, Vincent was right.

"Well, I thought I would try this one since it was new in Inheritance Bay."

Vincent snorted. "If you weren't my brother, I might believe that. If I didn't know how much of a snob you were in public, I might even have accepted your answer. However, since I know the truth of both of those statements, I think I'd like to know the real reason we are at this establishment."

Reid waved his hand in the air with a twenty-dollar bill in his hand, and a hostess found them. When they were seated, and Reid was looking at Vincent looking back at him, he put the menu down and looked at his brother.

"Vincent it's one dinner. Your internal organs will survive."

They placed their order, and then Vincent looked at Reid closely. Reid did his best not to squirm, but Vincent had a way about him.

"You know, Reid, I'm very popular right now in New York, and then you call me. Let's see how long it takes for me to figure it out what we are really doing here tonight."

In his desperation, Reid had paired himself up

with the brother who could figure out anything. Vincent was a person who had been hurt and was determined not to repeat the experience.

"I hear that you are getting ready to buy another company that—"

"So, we are going to do the small talk thing? I never thought I would do that with brothers but okay."

Reid shifted in his seat and took in the restaurant. They were seated in the back, but no one could come in or go out without Reid seeing them.

"You make it seem like we don't talk," Reid complained and then he heard it. It was Gloria's laugh. It was husky and rich. It was one of those authentic laughs where you knew the person was really enjoying themselves. Reid couldn't help himself; he dropped a napkin and when he bent down to pick it up, found Gloria with the mysterious man. The man leaned closer to her, and then she laughed again.

Reid wondered what could be so funny.

"Earth to Reid, come back. Reid, do you know that woman?" Vincent asked as he turned his chair around to look at Gloria and her date. When Vincent turned back, he looked at Reid and then started to sigh.

"You know it happens to the best of us. There is a siren out there who will test our convictions. This is your moment. Although, I have to admit, your test is much more attractive than most."

Reid heard Vincent's words and had to stop himself from grinding his teeth because Vincent was right. Reid was in a chain restaurant trying to size up the competition.

"The truth of the matter is I wanted to make sure this guy she was going out with was on the up and up."

Vincent took another look at Gloria and her companion.

"The man she's with looks very non-shady, Reid. In fact, I think I've seen him in the park, but I can't seem to remember where."

Reid didn't help his brother identify the companion. He was too busy looking for something that would make Gloria's companion appear less perfect.

Vincent turned and began to butter the bread that was brought to the table.

"That guy could make a living with those looks. I don't know, Reid; I think they're just fine. Reid didn't see it, but what did he know? The guy was sitting at dinner with Gloria, and he was watching her from afar. "You think he looks good?"

"That's Gloria Danvers."

Reid stopped looking at the couple and focused on Vincent.

"You know her?" Reid asked.

"She had a fundraiser. I think she was raising money for a yoga studio. She was very impressive," Vincent praised.

Reid wanted to beat his head against something. Now he knew what she needed the money for. If she had asked him, he would have given the money.

"Did you give to her cause?" Reid asked. He already knew the answer. Vincent didn't invest in anything that was dependent on people. He did technology and finance.

"No, but she almost had me convinced."

When the food arrived, Reid was conflicted about whether he should pour his shrimp scampi on Vincent's lap or go over to Gloria and tell her she didn't need to do another thing in her life because he would give her the money for the yoga. Then Reid heard what he was saying to himself. He was going to give her money, take care of her? What was he doing? She had told him to go away, and here he was, trying to think of a way to make her a princess.

"Come back, brother. Why don't you tell me what you know about her?" Vincent asked.

Reid was feeling like all types of a fool.

"Grayson hired her to help me review two of my new acquisitions."

"Is there something wrong with them, and if there is something wrong, shouldn't Kathy fix that?"

The questions were rapid fire just like Vincent. Reid ate a couple of the shrimp and had to admit Gloria was right. This place had good shrimp.

"It's nothing. She is doing a great job, and when she said she had a date tonight, I was a little concerned. It wasn't anything else."

Vincent paused for a moment and then laughed as he buttered up another slice of bread.

"So, If I am to believe you, we are sitting in a Salt and Brine because your intuition was set off when Gloria said she had a date tonight. On top of that, while you are giving me half answers about anything I ask you, you can't keep your eyes off of her."

"I'm scanning the room, not staring."

Vincent tsked him as he switched their plates. Reid watched as Vincent, after consuming the bread on the table and the food he'd ordered, was now about to eat Reid's as well.

"I want you to know that I make a habit of telling myself the truth, even if I have a different version that I give to everyone else. You need to find that truth and embrace it. If you are objectively looking over there, you will see that she is happy. She is smiling with him, and he's not making any sudden moves. She's not looking distressed. In fact, it looks like—"

"I get your point," Reid said. "So, you are right. The guy seems okay. I think—no, I know—they are close, and I wanted to see if it was the type of closeness that I should be concerned about."

Vincent clapped his hands.

Reid was confused. "You think this is something to celebrate?" Reid asked.

"I think that for a very long time you were just going through the motions, but you weren't really living. All of us have our demons to face. The way you face your demons is by putting your life on the line. I think you finding that you could care for someone have given you the pause you need."

"So, it looks like you've eaten all of the food, was that part of the punishment for me tonight?"

Vincent popped the last shrimp in his mouth.

"I had to eat, and eating here or eating in my office would have made no difference. However, I am a firm believer in opportunity. It would be rude of me to get up and leave this restaurant and not say hello to Gloria. After all, for me, this would be at a minimum the second time that I would have met Gloria in a public situation."

Then without Reid really understanding what

Vincent was going to do, Vincent stood up and went to say hello to Gloria and the mysterious Jack. Vincent was already across the hall, and he had called Gloria's name. Ironically, when she looked up, it wasn't Vincent who caught her eye. It was Reid. .

"Reid? Is that you?"

Then Vincent stepped in front of Reid and held his hand out to Gloria.

"You wouldn't believe how hard it is to get siblings to have dinner with you. I sometimes feel like I have to make an appointment in order to see my family."

The story wasn't ironclad, but it was enough for Gloria to know that his being here was an accident and not the result of some intense paranoia.

"Reid said he saw you on the side, and I wanted to be neighborly. Reid was telling me how you are working on his investments to make them organized so a child can run them."

The man known as Jack was smiling. When he heard she was helping redo the finances, a slow smile spread across his face and his hand covered hers on the table.

"I'm glad you are looking at finances again," he says. "It shows a lot of growth."

Gloria shook her head and told him it was nothing, and Reid was left wondering just who this Jack was and why his opinion was so important.

"I only considered it for the yoga studio."

"Well, I think if you are open to doing that type of work, I wouldn't mind giving to the rest of—" Reid watched Gloria place two fingers on his lips.

"Thank you, Jack, but no." Then Reid noticed that she could look at everyone in the conversation but him. He wanted to understand what was going on. Waiting was killing Reid, but he trusted his brother and knew he wouldn't let him down.

"I wanted you to know I was impressed with your presentation for the yoga studio. I'm not one into yoga, and if it were something that I normally acquired, then I would have joined."

"Thank you, it means a lot," Gloria said.

Vincent nodded his head toward Gloria.

"Well, we've taken up enough of your date night."

Jack held his hands up to get Vincent's attention. "Don't worry. This isn't a date. We're only catching up. I'm Jack Danvers, Gloria's brother."

Reid looked at Jack, and it all became clear. Now he could see how Jack and Gloria favored one another. To think he was jumping through hoops trying to follow her here.

"Who is the oldest out of you two?" Vincent asked.

Jack laughs. "I'm the older brother. I've always been looking out for her."

Reid looked at Gloria and she turned away, but his words about the man wanting to be the hero came back to him.. This wasn't the night he thought it would be, but it was the night he needed to decide if he was willing to take a risk or not. Reid stepped around Vincent and extended his hand to Jack.

"I'm Reid," he said. Reid could tell that Jack was waiting for him to reveal his relation to Gloria.

"I'm glad to meet you, Reid."

Should he introduce himself as her future husband? Looking at the anxious face on Gloria, that was probably a no. She wasn't ready for what he already knew.

"I'm the one who needs the idiot-proof plan on their finances," Reid said.

"You two are both a part of the Chance guys, right?"

Reid and Vincent nodded. Reid had never been so happy to be a Chance boy.

# CHAPTER 13

*G*loria knew that Jack wasn't going to let it go.

"I think it's great that you are able to take something you really love and find some good from it," Jack said. "There is also something going on between you and this Reid fellow."

Gloria sighed and just pushed her hands into her sweater pockets.

"It seems like everyone is really into putting labels on things all of a sudden. You don't have to name everything."

"Why are you so defensive? Is there something wrong with Reid?"

"No, he's well-to-do, a nice human being, and has a great sense of humor."

"Then he seems like a great candidate. More importantly, he seems to really like you. You need someone who will be patient."

Gloria shook her head.

"I don't need someone patient. I'm not going to

one day get up and forget that I lost a baby because my priorities were wrong. Don't you understand? I have what I deserve," Gloria said in a choked-up voice.

"You will recover. You are a young beautiful woman. You had a horrible experience, and you are so much richer for it. That doesn't mean you get to punish yourself for the rest of your life."

Gloria heard her brother, but the smell of iodine flooded her senses, and flashes of that time came back to her. How did one recover from taking an innocent through negligence? There were times when she thought that maybe she could find some peace, but the peace was short-lived. She had gone to the therapists and the group therapies to go over her form of survivor guilt. She had sat in a room of strangers and confessed as well as in a holy house, and still, there was a stain on her that she didn't think she could ever get rid of.

"I want you to get out there and live."

Gloria looked at her brother and let out a deep breath. It wasn't about fear. It was about worth. Gloria wasn't sure how it could be that an innocent baby wouldn't make it into the world. However, in the next scene, she was living fine. Things didn't make sense. It didn't make sense for them, and she didn't think it made sense now. She had decided to not try to figure things out anymore. When she opened her studio, she'd be doing good for those who were the most vulnerable. Maybe after some time went by, she'd feel worthy enough to get a life on her own. Explaining that to Jack wasn't even an option, and that truth isolated her from him as well.

Gloria could see that Jack wasn't going to let this go.

"Reid doesn't know everything. I am working on it, and that's what we've agreed on, right?"

Jack smiled and then shook his head. "You know that I went along with the plan because I thought I could help you," Jack said with a bit more heat in his voice.

"Help me? You have helped me. You've been there for me no matter that problem or the issue," Gloria said.

"I know, but I can see now that it was a crutch."

"Jack, how can you say this? Don't let Reid's words make you regret what we have. He doesn't understand how much I needed, and you gave it without hesitation."

Jack let out a heavy sigh.

"I gave it to you because that was all I had. I gave it to you because I loved you, but I also gave it to you because I needed to know that I could do something as well."

Then like a slow train wreck, it was dawning on Gloria that Reid was right.

"You know I love you, right, Jack?"

"I know academically that you do, but I've always felt that the times you've needed me, I've failed you."

"Jack?!!"

"Listen, when I was traveling the world to be a world-class chef, you were doing policy and financing. When our mother was still mourning, you had to be everything to her. I didn't come home; it wasn't like I couldn't. I just didn't want to face not being able to do anything but endure her pain.

Those meetings with her on Dad's death anniversary were torture. I felt like a failure every equinox. Then when Mom passed away, I could tell you some of the good stories about when Dad was around. The dinners changed. I was able to make it a safe place for you. I was able to make it someplace you wanted to come. It was rough for us all, but I could give you some good times and I felt like I was doing my part as your big brother and making it safe for you."

Gloria didn't know what to say.

"Tonight was the first time I saw you happy in your current space. I've been giving you memories to hold on to, but Reid has a future for you. I think the both of us have grown. I don't need to be the hero in your life anymore. I'm in a different place in my life where I feel secure. I love you so much that when I saw the way you reacted to Reid, I knew he was the one for you."

There was a moment of silence after he spoke when neither of them said anything. Gloria looked up at Jack, and the words don't come. Jack, on the other hand, called the waitress over and paid the bill.

"Do you want to go home now?"

Gloria looked at him and shook her head.

"I get it. Look. I'm going to stay somewhere else tonight," Jack said.

"I don't want to put you out of your place."

"No, it's fine. I need some time to think. I have my own bedroom, but I didn't want you to feel crowded tonight."

Gloria moves the food around on the plate for about fifteen minutes and then decided it was time to leave. The good news about being in a small town was that most things were within walking distance.

Tonight, Gloria really needed the walk. She never looked at things the way Jack had told them to her tonight. She had always leaned on Jack, and when their mother passed, it was true Jack was able to recreate the past and she was able to have a father without having had the time that Jack had with him.

Reid was right. Jack had been and still was her hero. Jack thought it was just for the days when they got together to remember their parents, but he was wrong. He was always her hero. Now Gloria felt lower than the belly of a snake. She had given Reid the cold shoulder and had discounted his feelings and his insights. Now she knew that she was the one who had a narrow view. She still wasn't sure what she was going to do about the feeling of inadequacy. She believed in love, but it was hard to feel worthy.

She went home, and the first thing she wanted to do was see Reid. She wasn't sure what was going on, but she was sure that Reid was a part of it. The problem was she had basically told Reid that they weren't an item anymore, and for once, he had listened to her.

*DINNER?*

*WHO IS THIS?*

Gloria smiled. Reid knew who it was.

*WOW, DOES THE CALLER ID NOT WORK?*

*OH, GLORIA.*

*DINNER?*

*ME? YOU WANT TO GO TO DINNER WITH ME? WHAT KIND OF DINNER IS THIS? ARE WE DISCUSSING BUSINESS?*

*THIS IS THE LAST TIME. TAKE IT OR LEAVE IT, DINNER?*

*DONE!*

*GOOD. I'LL SEND THE TIME AND PLACE. SEE YOU TOMORROW.*

∼

*ARE YOU UP?*

Kathy looked at the text from Gloria and let out a sigh of relief. She wasn't sure what Reid had done, but whatever it was, things were moving in the right direction again.

*Of course, I'M UP FOR YOU. HOW ARE YOU?*

*I THINK I MESSED THINGS UP TODAY, BUT I'VE FIXED IT.*

Kathy wanted to shake her head and say don't try to fix anything on your own, but she knew Gloria wouldn't appreciate it.

*NOT YOU- WHAT HAPPENED?*

*FIRST, I PUSHED REID AWAY. THEN I MET JACK WHO SAID REID WAS RIGHT AND THEN I INVITED HIM TO DINNER FOR TOMORROW.*

Kathy fell back on her bed and wondered how two people who were fated for each other couldn't get it right. If the two of them, who were so obviously right for each other, were having problems, it was no wonder that everyone else was having an issue. Although Kathy was going to give them a break because things would have gone very nicely if it weren't for that Jack guy.

*SO, ARE YOU GOING TO BE DRESSING UP, OR IS THIS BUSINESS CASUAL?*

*LOL WE WILL NOT BE TALKING ABOUT INVESTMENTS, SO CASUAL*

*GOOD GIRL*

*I DO HAVE TO FINISH THIS PLAN.*

*WHY DON'T YOU COME FINISH IT HERE AND THEN WE CAN HANG OUT*

*HANG OUT?*

*YOU DON'T WANT TO HANG OUT WITH A GOOD GUY LIKE ME*

*FOR YOU I MIGHT*

*WOW, YOU HAVE BEEN HANGING AROUND REID TOO LONG, TAKING RISKS!*

*OR MAYBE REID HAS BEEN HANGING AROUND ME.*

Kathy closed her phone and shook her head. The both of them were beyond stubborn. She couldn't wait for them to get it together. Then she could be sure that Reid was in good hands. She'd think about what she was going to do from that point on. Kathy heard Reid when he said that she could stay, but she also knew that no one wanted to have a third wheel around.

# CHAPTER 14

*W*hy do people go on dates past the age of eighteen?

Reid was standing in front of Gloria's house in a nice neighborhood that just screamed settled down. The manicured lawns and the kid toys on the front lawn advertised what kind of people were here. The question was, did Reid feel like he could become one of these people?

He got ready to knock on the door, and Gloria pulled it open. He had to keep his mouth closed because her hair was down. It was glorious. Long sable curls danced around her waist. She had on blue jeans and a powder pink top that had delicate ruffles along the arm. Reid wasn't one to really pay attention to fashion, but he was paying attention to Gloria.

"I'm glad you made it and on time. I was just coming outside," Gloria said.

"I do learn," Reid said. It was better that she think he learned than she knew that he was so nervous to go on this date that he was ready about three hours ago. "So, my lady, where are we going?" He was waiting for her to pick some delicate place where salad was considered one of the main courses.

"I made reservations at The Standard. It's a steak place, but I thought it would be more your speed."

Reid smiled. "When I'm in town, it's my favorite place to go. Already, you are showing that you know the me that I don't usually show others."

"Okay, it's not that serious, but thank you. Jack likes this place as well," Gloria said.

Just like that, at the mention of her brother, Reid was not as jovial.

"Do you two come here a lot?" he asked, trying to show that he had indeed grown.

"Not really. This is a place we come to when we have hit a milestone." When Reid heard her words he thought maybe going there was a good idea, after all. He wouldn't mind being considered a milestone in Gloria's life. He was so deep in contemplation he didn't hear something that Gloria said.

"Hey, I'm sorry, I won't mention my brother tonight."

Reid smiled. "It's someone we need to address because you can't send him back and get a new one."

Gloria smiled, and Reid sighed. That was a close one, having to deal with his feelings about Jack. When they got to the restaurant and took their seats, Reid watched Gloria look over the menu. He smiled to himself at the thought that she was the one who picked the venue, but she still needed to look at the menu. When she had made up her mind, she found him looking at her.

"I know, you would think since I picked the spot, I'd know what I wanted, but it's not true. Thank you for your patience."

"So here we are on a date, and we aren't going to be talking about business," Reid said.

Gloria looked at Reid, and he knew if something didn't change soon his chance was going to be gone.

"I guess it's time to ask all the special date questions that you can only ask when you first meet a person," Reid said.

"Okay, I'm game," Gloria said eagerly.

"Five years from now, how many children will we have?" Reid asked.

Gloria's eyes popped open, and then she started laughing.

"Now I can take that as we will not have any children or that we'll have so many you don't know if you can tell me, and I still stay around."

"Reid, stop it! Who asks that anymore?"

"As a man, I need to know how many mouths I have to feed," he said indignantly.

"Well, I'm thinking I want an even number," Gloria said, looking into the air.

"True, they have to come in pairs so they can take care of each other. Good thinking," Reid praised.

"Take care of each other?" Gloria echoed.

"You know steps take care of child below them. So, if they come in pairs and you're in good health now, right?"

"Yes, I am but—"

"Good, then you can have kids until you are in

your late sixties, I think the research says. I think a good number would be like eight. If we're lucky, you'll have duplicates. Your thoughts?"

"Eight! Isn't that a sports team of some kind?"

"Maybe, but not all of the kids will be into sports," Reid said.

"I know, but eight?"

"What we have to think about is attrition," Reid said as he watched Gloria cover her mouth in surprise. That was the beginning of a great night. From that point on, the food was brought, and it was eaten while lively conversation was had. This was what Reid had imagined when he thought of a date with Gloria. He made sure she ate throughout the night. When dessert came, they opted to share a plate. When the black-and-white fudge cake was brought out, Reid took the opportunity to feed Gloria. At first, Gloria hesitated.

"Reid?"

"Trust me, Gloria."

During dessert, Reid was aware of every movement that Gloria made. This was the woman that he wanted to share the rest of his life with. It came to him like a whisper. With each one of her laughs, it became the truth that he couldn't deny. Gloria Danvers was the woman he wanted to spend all of his tomorrows with. After he paid the check, they walked hand in hand with each other. Reid felt like he did when he completed his first deal and made a profit. Reid felt invincible. When they get to her home, he opened the car door and walked her slowly to her door as if it were their first date.

She turned to face him, and he could see her lick her bottom lip as she looked for words.

"Don't fret, princess. I'm not looking to come in. I know you have a protector that would be more than happy to have an excuse to do me bodily harm,"

"Jack isn't like that."

"He wasn't until his baby sister found the man of her dreams."

"Oh, so now you are the man of my dreams? You are really sure about yourself."

Read reached out with a hand and traced her cheek.

"I'm not sure about me. I'm sure about us."

Reid leaned down and watched as her eyes closed. When he was a hair's breadth away from her lips, he took in her scent. Gloria always had the faint aroma of lavender around her. Then she exhaled as if giving him a cue to kiss her. Reid pressed his lips to hers and knew she was the one he'd been waiting for. She was the one worth taking a chance on love again. She was the one.

When the kiss ended, Reid didn't tell her the discovery he'd made. Instead, Reid smiled at her.

"I'm thinking we need to practice this dating thing," he said with a smile.

She nodded and smiled back at him.

"Text me, Reid. I mean, I want to be ready to do some more practicing."

"Of course."

Reid watched Gloria go into the house. He wanted to pull her into his arms and kiss her again, but he had to remember he was playing the long game for keeps.

# CHAPTER 15

*T*he text came like clockwork, and Gloria was ecstatic. She showered and prepared herself for a day with Reid. Then she checked her schedule; for today it said, *Liz's birthday*.

What was wrong with her? How could she have forgotten it was her taken too soon baby's birthday? She should have been home instead of hanging out with Reid. A migraine started from the pressure, and she considered not doing a thing to stop it. She probably deserved it.

This was all Reid's doing. Practice dating? What kind of cheesy line was that? More importantly, how could she fall for that cheesy line? Gloria was surprised that Jack wasn't in her room already. What was she going to do? She needed to make some decisions. Gloria picked up the phone.

"Reid, I can't go with you today."

"Wow, you thought about it and decided that no amount of practice would help?" he said jokingly, but she could hear the tension in his voice.

"It's not that at all. I had an appointment for today that I need to keep."

"It's no problem. You know dating isn't just about dinners, desserts, and hanging out with an amazing guy. Dating is also about doing mundane things together. I'll take you."

Gloria closed her eyes. Why did he have to be so sweet now?

"This isn't an errand like that, and most of the time Jack takes me."

"Okay, is this another Jack-only party, and I have to wait until I get my membership approved?"

Gloria closed her eyes. On the one hand, she understood why Reid felt left out. It wasn't fair to him, especially after last night. If she were honest, this was about her and not Reid. Doing this said something, and it meant there was no turning back.

"Your membership is approved, Reid. Why don't you come by in an hour?"

"You got it."

As if things just couldn't get any more complicated. When Gloria hung up the phone with Reid, Jack popped his head into the room.

"Hey, what time do you want me to drop you off today?"

He looked neutral but cheerful. Gloria didn't know what is harder: saying no to him or taking Reid?

"I'm not going to need a ride."

Jack came into the room and had a concerned look on his face.

"Hey, you don't have to do this on your own, you know. I told you when you came, I'd always be here."

Gloria walked into Jack's arms and hugged him

tight. Then when she decided she could look at him without crying, she stepped away.

"I'm not going alone."

He looked at her confused for a moment, and then he nodded.

"Reid"

"Yes, Reid is going to drive me today."

He pulled back and gave her a long look. "Did you tell him?"

"I told him, but I didn't tell him where I was going today."

"That's not like you, Gloria," Jack admonished.

Gloria wanted to rail at him and say she knew it wasn't not like her. She wanted to say to him she knew this wasn't her regular way of handling things, but surely this situation was an exception.

"I know, but I'm winging it."

Jack stroked her hair and then gave it a little tug.

"Hey, brat, remember I'm your brother. I beat up bad guys, and I stand by your side if you need it."

Gloria knew Jack would always be there for her. It was nice to know that they both agreed on the premise of him being her support no matter what.

"I'll remember. Now I have to get my gear. Thanks, Jack."

Gloria texted Reid. She wanted him to be at her house in thirty minutes. Reid arrived in twenty. Gloria grabbed her photo and went into the refrigerator to get the snack she was bringing for the event. Gloria packed it all into a bag and then ran out to a curious Reid. As he came around the car, she watched this man with whom she has decided to give love a try. She has a flashback of Davis, but she knew that Reid wasn't Davis. Reid was trustworthy and they talked about things. They didn't have secrets and personal agendas.

"Thanks for coming and changing plans on such short notice."

"It's no problem. You are the most important person to me. I think everyone else can hold up for you."

As Gloria got into the car she commented, "I take it you are used to having people wait on you?"

Reid shrugged. "I can't say I even notice. Everyone usually doesn't have a problem."

Gloria laughed as he closed the door. She needed Reid's moments of levity and humor in her life.

When he got into the car, Gloria handed him the address. He looked at what she was carrying and then back at her. He turned his attention to the road. Gloria was glad because it was all she could do to keep it together. The trip took shorter than Gloria could think. Of course, it did. This was the day that she was with Reid. She hadn't said anything, but it was all clear when they pulled up to the cemetery.

"Gloria," Mr. Stone greeted. Mr. Stone has been kind to Gloria from day one. It was Jack's idea that she have a burial plot. He said it would allow Gloria closure, and it did. "I replaced the flowers for you. Is Jack coming?"

"Jack isn't coming today. My friend Reid is here with me today."

Mr. Stone looked Reid up and down and then gave a grunt.

"He'll do. It looks like he is a bit thin. Bring him up to the main house, and we will fix him yet. It's hard to understand why men are scared of a little weight. In my day, if a man had some weight on him, he was going to do some work. All in all, he's a good man for you."

Gloria had to hang her head to hide her smile. It amazed Gloria how Mr. Stone had come to the same conclusion she had but in such a shorter time.

"He's not my man, Mr. Stone."

Mr. Stone shook his head. "Back in my day, people didn't do personal stuff together unless they belonged to each other."

Reid stepped forward and held out his hand. "Hello, Mr. Stone. I'm Reid, and I'm her man. Her brother was bringing her up until I got up to speed. I'll make sure she gets to and fro with no problem."

Gloria said nothing. Her man. Is that what Reid was now? Gloria wanted to correct him but there was nothing wrong with it and she didn't want to cause a scene. At least that was what she told herself, this was about image. Gloria ignored the racing of her heart and the way her feelings were all over the place.

They started the walk up the path. It was a bit steep, but if the flowers were good it would be beautiful. Gloria walked on in silence, and that was when she saw that the flowers had been replaced and renewed. There was a bench by the small headstone in the ground. It was past time. She went to the bench and faced Reid who has also taken a seat.

"This was where I created a final resting place for Elizabeth Danvers. When I had come here, my brother asked what had happened after the miscarriage. I told him what always happens, they told me it had happened. They sent in a grief counselor and at the time Davis, a guy from an old relationship, had come by to tell me to throw myself into my work to forget. It turned out, that I didn't forget. In fact, I started to have nightmares and trouble concentrating on my work. When I realized that I was making rookie mistakes in setting up a portfolio, I knew I needed to do something.

Anyway, the something, according to my brother, was to create a final resting place for her so that I would be able to find some kind of closure. Before I got this plot, I would have nightmares of her wandering around not sure that she was loved or that she belonged. This plot fixed those issues for me."

"The food?" Reid asked.

"I used to bake. I learned just for her. So, I bring a snack that I've made. It's silly but there it is."

Reid pulled Gloria into his arms. Her quiet tears fell onto his shoulders. Hopefully he didn't mind. She knew he could feel her quiet tears on his shoulders.

"No one knows how amazing you are. You have your own hurts and pains, but you don't let those spill into other people's lives," Reid said. This ritual she has to honor her daughter is tasteful and is another example of her loving nature. Reid couldn't have done better finding a woman to take a chance with.

"I want to thank you, Gloria. Thank you for sharing this with me. I am honored, and I want you to know that I won't betray your trust."

From that point on, they both prepared the ground by wiping away errant leaves on the plot and taking a seat on the grass so they could eat the small snack. Forty-five minutes later, the snack was over, and they were walking back to the car.

Reid grabbed ahold of Gloria's hand, and the

day didn't seem as heavy. With a simple touch she didn't feel so alone in this moment. When they got to the car, Gloria had tears running down her face. She knew this was part of the healing process, but today she wasn't alone.

"I miss my baby. I know they'll say all sorts of medical things. They gave me all the reasons why these things happen. All I could hear was my baby was gone.

The worst of it is I felt like I had done something. I mean if they couldn't tell me what had happened, then they couldn't rule out anything."

"I can't say I have any experience in this. I can't even begin to imagine the pain you went through, Gloria. What I can say is that I'm here now. If you need anything, please lean on me. I think we can leave here and go somewhere else. I know a great space in the pond."

"Okay," Gloria said. She would have agreed to just about anything. She just wanted to not make any decisions and to leave. Reid provided the solution to both of them.

# CHAPTER 16

he next Monday, Gloria and Reid were in a limousine. Reid has already said they were going to look at his second property. Reid hadn't found a way to explain his second property to Gloria. He knew that she'd think that something is off, but she couldn't tell what it was. The first problem was that the property was supposed to be in Westchester. The truth of the matter was that the property was sitting in Smithtown. As they drove in the limousine, Gloria flipped through the very small file on the property.

After their visit to the cemetery, he knew he could share this secret with her. It seemed as though knowing you could do something and actually doing it were two different things. Reid's heart had been racing all throughout the trip. It wasn't making it any easier than this morning when a file was delivered to his room. He could always count on his brother Vincent to go and research every single person.

Sitting in a manila folder in his briefcase was a

record of everything that Gloria had ever done. The file wasn't very big, but it was just big enough for Reid to have some kind of curiosity. When he had gotten back to his room, the manila folder was on top of his bed with a note that said *Merry Christmas*.

Trust was a very big thing between him and Gloria. If he looked inside the manila folder, he would break that trust. When he thought about Gloria and how she was at the cemetery, he just couldn't do it. If there was going to be any chance for them in a relationship, Gloria would have to tell him all of her secrets. He didn't want to read about the secret details of her life. Reid wanted Gloria to feel comfortable enough to share all of the real problems with him.

"Okay, I give. Where are we going?" Gloria asked.

"We are going to my other investment."

"It says it's in Westchester."

"It's legally set up in that county, but it is not there. It's in Smithtown. It's not making a profit, and I'm still keeping it. Let me be clear, it may never make a profit, but I'd still want to keep it."

Reid could see he had surprised Gloria. Her little black folder was closed, and she was looking at him expectantly. He had expected her to be upset or to show some sort of reaction that would have been very appropriate. Instead, she was sitting across from him just waiting.

"So, this project is one of the heart?" Gloria asked.

Reid hadn't thought about it, but that would be a true statement. Reid wished he could explain to her how important this investment was to him. Gloria leaned forward and crooked her finger toward him. Reid leaned forward.

"You are getting nervous for nothing. I care about everything you care about. If you know this investment isn't making a profit and you still want to keep it, fine. We can go look at it, but we won't assess it. Is that okay?" Gloria asked. Reid was dumbfounded, and he nodded. Then he leaned forward and kissed her.

"I don't know what I did to deserve you," Reid said.

"I don't know either, but maybe you can make it up to me by spoiling me outrageously," she said with a smile.

Reid leans forward and kissed her. Now that his stomach had settled, and Gloria had made it clear that she understood that this was not a money-making event, the stress was taken from his shoulders.

"No problem. Let me know what you want, and I'll work on getting it to you as soon as possible."

Gloria laughed, and the sound made Reid feel like a king. She was a beautiful woman inside and out who was vulnerable and strong. It was rare that he saw that type of strength. Kathy had that kind of strength. Reid had never expected to find that in a woman who would be interested in him.

"You are stalling. Tell me about the property."

"So, a couple of years back I had an accident. Okay, that isn't so rare, but this one was because I had fallen backward down a ski slope. It wasn't anything with my back or walking, but I was going to be bedbound for a while. Someone had suggested service animals because my spirits were down. Then they brought me a dog, and it was nice but not enough.

Eventually, they wound up taking me to a farm where they had horses. I discovered that I knew nothing about horses. When I was able to walk again, I realized that horse therapy was an absolutely horrible business. It seemed as though having a horse therapy farm was a no-brainer for losing money. Every time I got ready to ask someone who had a horse therapy farm how they make ends meet, and they all said they had a second job.

The good news is I don't need to get a second job. However, this farm will always be at a loss. I know that isn't what Grayson will want to hear, but this is important to me, so I don't want to give it up.

Gloria leaned over and gave him a chaste kiss.

"Stop fretting. I understand how important this is, and I want you to know I'll look at it based on merit, not the bottom-line numbers."

"But—"

"Trust me, Reid."

For the rest of the trip, Reid was silent. How could he be anything but when Gloria had just asked him to do the same thing she had?

According to Reid, everything was going great, and Kathy couldn't be happier. This is what she wanted for her brother. She wanted him to know what it meant to be in love, and Reid and Gloria were almost at the church. Life was going great until Kathy got a text from Vincent.

*WE NEED TO MEET FOR DINNER. REID IS*

*IN TROUBLE.*

Why, oh, why did Vincent have to distrust everything?

*I SPOKE TO HIM NOT LONG AGO. HE'S GOOD.*
*MEET ME, KATHY, OR I'LL MOBILIZE*
*EVERYONE TO HELP HIM.*
*TWO HOURS AT THE DINER.*

The threat of mobilizing the brothers was no idle one, and Kathy knew better than to push Vincent. The problem with having people who love you was that they didn't have limits when it came to protecting you. Two hours later, they were in a diner. Of course, Vincent was already there. He was on a crusade.

Vincent looked like he was already annoyed, tapping a manila folder against his black jeans. He had on a blue shirt that looked like it was painted on, and his hair was so long now that he could be a recovering hippie in all of the right ways.

The waitress followed Kathy to her table because, like all of the Chance brothers, Vincent was attractive.

"Is there anything I can get for you?"

What she really meant was, is there anything she could get for Vincent?

"No, thank you." Any hope of an appetite had gone by the wayside when she saw the determined look in Vincent's eyes.

"What is it?"

"Wow, I can't call you out for some brunch?"

"No, its never that simple, you are always troubling, Vincent."

"I am not the problem. I just happen to find problems."

Vincent pushed the envelope across the table.

"I think that someone should look into these envelopes to make sure that Gloria is the woman she says she is."

"No."

One could try to ignore Vincent, but that wasn't easily done. Protecting Gloria and Reid could be done, and Kathy had every intention of doing so. Vincent got a hamburger with French fries. He separated his fries and then cut his burger up into six slices. When he finished eating, he once again pushed the envelope to Kathy.

"You can start anytime you want," Kathy said.

"I don't need to say anything. I think we need to look in the folder and make some judgments. Reid is vulnerable, and I would think you of all people would want to make sure no one takes advantage of him."

It took everything inside of Kathy to listen to Vincent and not tell him what she really thought. Vincent had always been very good at making judgments. Kathy listened to Vincent's conclusions for the next thirty minutes. He hadn't said anything that Reid and Kathy didn't already know. As Kathy listened to Vincent, she was very happy that she'd decided to come out and try to nip this catastrophe waiting to happen in the bud. Long ago, Kathy had learned that the art of dealing with Vincent was to let him run his course.

"What exactly would you like me to do about this right now, Vincent?"

"I would think that is obvious. Reid will listen to you. You just need to tell him to get rid of this girl."

"And I'm supposed to get rid of her because of

all of the research that you've done?"

"These are the facts. I thought you wanted to look out for what was best for Reid."

"You haven't even met her."

Vincent tapped the folder on the table. "I don't need to meet her. I know everything about her."

"I need you to tell me what's really bothering you."

"I just think it's very coincidental that her ex-fiancé happens to be one of our competitors when it comes to investments."

Kathy wanted to laugh at Vincent's paranoia.

"So, you think that she was sent as a spy to get Reid?"

"Listen, I've met her, and I know that doesn't count for a lot on your part, but let me tell you, she's human and she's had a lot of trauma lately. If you want to know if she is the one for Reid, I think you need to take some time and spend it with them."

"I sent you a copy."

"Of?"

"Of whom she is?"

Kathy had heard enough. "Vincent, keep your folder to yourself. I think if you took the time to talk to her, you would have a different point of view."

Vincent stood up, upset. "When he finds himself folding sheets in hotels and she's taken all of his money, then you'll come back to me and say you should have listened."

With that, Vincent got up and left. Kathy sat there and picked at her fries. The only thing she could do now was hope that Reid and Gloria moved this show along before their well-meaning family got in the way.

# CHAPTER 17

*S*omething was wrong with Reid. He hadn't called since she gave in the report to Grayson. She thought after them seeing the horses in Smithtown that maybe things were different, but she was wrong.

Today she was waiting for him to come over to do a review of the final report. She'd already done a preliminary, but she always offered another review, and Reid wanted one. He finally arrived at the house, and he looked beyond harried.

"Are you sure you don't want to do our final meet at one of my places?" Reid asked. Gloria was mildly offended. Was there something wrong with her place? Gloria didn't know what was wrong with Reid, but she did know that he was not acting like his normal self.

"It's a beautiful day outside. Gloria, are you sure you don't want us to go do this someplace where we can get some sun?"

What was wrong with him? First he wanted to

see her, then he didn't want to see her at her house. Now he wanted to go outside. She just didn't have whatever it took to keep up with all he was going through.

"No, I think we should stay in the house and take care of this so that you can go on your way, and I can go mine."

He looked like a petulant little boy as he went to the kitchen table and plopped down into his seat. Gloria went into the kitchen and turned back to Reid. She was not sure what was wrong, but she was going to have to bring it up somehow. Smoothing her hands on the side of her pants, she turned around right into Reid's arms. Then without warning, he kissed her.

"Okay, what is that for?"

"I am celebrating our third date," Reid said.

"The third date? This is the second."

"We have to count the time we went to see the horses because there was no business going on that day."

Gloria looked at Reid and thought he was crazy.

"Why does it even matter how many dates we've been on?"

"It matters, so I don't seem presumptuous."

Gloria was still confused. "Reid, would you tell me already because I don't know what you are trying to say, and it's driving me crazy."

Reid placed a kiss on Gloria's lips. "I love you, Gloria. I have always thought you were full of spit and fire. I've learned that you are also full of possibilities and your compassion makes you a safe haven for others. You make me realize that there is more to life than money. I've learned that my most prized business isn't a business at all but my family. I always knew I loved my family, but you helped me to see family in a new light. Looking at you with Kathy has also opened my eyes that maybe she needs more than just me. Looking on while you deal with your grief and come to some kind of closure has shown me how strong you are as a woman. You inspire me. I love you inside and out, and I couldn't think of a time without you. Will you marry me, Gloria Danvers?"

Gloria was completely taken aback. Of course, she knew that they were getting closer and that their relationship was moving on, but this? After they had gone to see the horses and had gone to the cemetery, their relationship changed. She had some doubts about him being rich and her not, but the most important thing was that he loved her. He loved her, and he wanted to marry her. It was a rollercoaster ride that would be Reid Chance, but she could manage that.

He was waiting, and Gloria was thinking.

Reid was a good man. He wasn't cruel or mean to others. He treated others who didn't make as much as him with respect and kindness. He loved his family and his sister. He was faithful and compassionate. His brothers were a bit much, but they all loved him. Most of all, he was flexible, and he loved her.

Who turned down marriage to a man who was independently wealthy and who wanted to give you the world?

"Yes!"

"Yes!" Reid echoed. "You won't regret this." He laughed. He picked her up and twirled her around.

"I know that Grayson and Rose are planning their wedding. How about we get married before them? I want you to have your day all to yourself."

"I do want to have a wedding all to myself, but I don't want to rush things," Gloria said.

"We aren't going to rush. I'm thinking we can get married in two months, around Christmas."

Christmas? It was so soon, Gloria thought. She loved him, so why shouldn't she? They knew all there was to know about each other. She needed to explain Davis in depth, but that was a small thing, all things considered. She realized Reid was waiting.

"I'll consider Christmas."

Reid jumped for joy. "I'm going to have to let the board know so there isn't a hoopla."

Gloria had a weird feeling in her stomach. "You have to tell your business that you are going to get married?"

"It's a preliminary. They want to make sure I haven't signed away their jobs. Don't worry. My business just wants to make sure I haven't been taken against my will and that I'm still of sound body and mind."

"Wow, I never thought marrying me could translate to you being crazy," Gloria said. The door opened, and in came Jack.

"I guess it is fitting that you are the first one to know. Gloria has done me the honor of agreeing to be my wife," Reid said to Jack. Gloria could see the moment of hesitation in his eyes before he smiled and congratulated them both. Gloria hadn't realized she was holding her breath until both of them were shaking hands. She needed both of these men in her life. They started talking and Reid said he and Jack were going out. Gloria waved them off and had to call her bestie. Although, the way Portia was sometimes, she expected Portia to call her and tell her she was about to marry money.

"Portia?"

"Oh, so you remember your little plebian friend." She sniffed on the phone.

"I am calling you first," Gloria said.

"First?"

"I mean, if you don't want to know—"

"Tell me! I can decide if your news makes up for the blatant abuse you have put me through."

"Reid asked me to marry him, and I said yes."

"I knew it! I knew it! I want the first child named after me. I am so happy for you. I don't know what to do."

"My firstborn? Wow, I'm glad we're not asking for anything big," Gloria said with a smile sarcastically.

"Okay, maybe not the first but at least the second!"

"I called to let you know because I could just imagine you holding it against me the rest of my life if I didn't."

"You would be right. Well, this wedding should be filled with eligible men who are looking for their princesses as well," Portia said.

"I have no idea who will come, but we'll know when we write up the list of who is who. Also, take into consideration people may not be able to come because it may be at Christmas."

"Why so quick?"

"He thinks that's late. His idea was to marry next week."

"Next week! No, no, no. My friend is going to get the royal treatment. I don't know if Christmas is enough time for people to arrange to come."

"Well, when your man is the local hunk and the man with more dollars than the local bank, you will find that people want to come to the wedding," Portia said.

"Do you really care about the money?"

"I don't care about money, but I have to tell you that I can't work all of my life. Now tell me the juicy part. What does the ring look like? Can you land a plane with it?"

"Well, he didn't have a ring. I think he came over just for us to go over his final packet, and then something made him pop the question."

"Made him pop the question?" Portia repeated.

"It's not a big deal. I'll send you a pic as soon as we pick out a ring," Gloria said.

"Well until my prince charming comes or I go out there and hunt him down, you are going to have to do this up right. So let the spending begin and the fairy tale start spinning."

# CHAPTER 18

*T*rying to fix once-in-a-lifetime moments was problematic.

Reid realized he had a problem. He had proposed to his fiancée in her house. He didn't even have the decency to have a ring. If there was going to be any chance of salvaging this, he was going to have to do the proposal all over again. Reid invited Gloria to his starter home where they had peanut butter cookies. He was comfortable, and then they could use the home as the place to start their family.

When she came over, Reid had prepared breakfast for her. He had a service come into the home and clean it, and right now it looked as if he had spent all night making it the perfect place for her. The air was refreshed, the lavender sachets were everywhere.

Reid couldn't have done the cleaning to the place because he had been running around like a chicken with his head cut off trying to get it all together. He had to offer a very large bonus to get a jeweler to get up and modify a piece that would be worthy of Gloria.

After getting a ring, Reid had several other pieces made. They would all match the ring, and he hoped the sheer number would make it seem like he had some forethought, and they weren't just made.

Reid asked Gloria to go out and get the mail because he was waiting for something and then he took the opportunity to lay out all the jewelry. When she came back into the room, she gasped and ran into Reid's arms. Then he pulled her away and hinted to the eggs behind him.

"Breakfast is cold."

Gloria groaned. "Breakfast compared to this."

"There's more, so you need to keep your strength up."

"I'm good."

Reid pulled Gloria into his arms and just inhaled her hair. Then he stepped back.

"The boxes are here, and I'll take you anywhere you want to get a ring you want. I realized that I did this wrong. I wanted to have flowers and to do it up, so you'd remember it as a great romantic moment, but instead, I rushed and I wanted to try to make it better for you."

Gloria looked at him and then leaned in and kissed him.

"Reid, I'm so happy I don't know what to do. The way you asked me is just fine for us. It may not have been with flowers and such, but I know it was sincere and that you love me. I think that's really all that matters."

Reid frowned and looked at her and the boxes.

"The jeweler boxes are all yours. They go with your eyes," Reid said, and Gloria started laughing.

"I don't think there is any jewelry on the planet that goes with my eyes but thank you so much for saying that. Why don't you take a seat, and I'll serve us some breakfast?"

Reid nodded and went into the bathroom. Everything was the way it should be. He would call Kathy tonight and let her know Gloria was fine. When Reid went back into the dining room Gloria was there, trying to clear off the chairs so they could sit. She picked up his duffle bag and a manila envelope fell out. Reid saw it and remembered it was the folder from Vincent. He tried to get to it, but as fate would have it Gloria gets it first.

"What is this?" she asked.

Reid wondered what he could say that would even dissuade her. When she turned it over and it had her name on it, there was little chance that anything would dissuade her. This was one of those times when Reid was thinking that Vincent's paranoia could be a challenge.

"Would you believe me if I told you it was nothing?"

Gloria picked up the folder and looked at it on both sides.

"If it's nothing, how come it has my name on it?" Then before Reid could give an explanation, she pulled out a sheet.

"This is about me?"

Reid got ready to explain. He wanted to explain how the report was just sitting in his bag and how he was never going to use it, but he hadn't gotten around to throwing it away"

"So how long have you had it?"

Reid wanted to answer but he saw the hurt in her eyes and there was nothing he could think of to make it go away.

"I was offered it before we went to the farm."

"So did you find anything interesting in it?"

Reid saw her fold her arms over her chest, and he knew this was a losing battle.

"Gloria, I didn't read it."

"So, after you received this then I was okay to marry?" she asked in a low whisper.

Reid walked toward her, and then Gloria walked back.

"It's not like that. You know my brother is a bit overboard about not trusting people."

"I do know, but I'm wondering why you didn't just tear up the report?"

"I didn't get a chance to do it! Gloria, what is the problem here?"

"The problem here is that I thought we both were trusting each other. It turns out that only I was trusting, and you didn't need to."

"I didn't look at the report."

"It's not just the report. It's the fact you didn't tell me either. I might have been able to look over the one, but both of them? I took you to Elizabeth's grave. I shared with you without a report or any type of background check to see how much money you have or looking to see what is in your background. For trust to work, it's a two-way street."

"I know that, and I trust you."

"What made you ask me to marry you?

"I love you! We are right when we are together. Can't you see—"

"I can see that our ideas of trust are different, and if those are different, then our ideas on rent will be different too. Listen, I have to have some space."

"Let's talk it out, Gloria—"

"I can't talk to you now."

Gloria gathered her purse and left out of the door. Reid could do nothing but watch her go. When it was clear she was not coming back, he texted Kathy.

*SHE'S GONE*

*WHAT?*

*I DON'T KNOW WHAT HAPPENED. SHE'S GONE.*

Reid felt gutted, and there wasn't even an enemy to fight. Whatever it was he knew it was big but without communication, there was no way that he could address it.

*COME HOME.*

*I'M NOT GOOD COMPANY NOW.*

*COME HOME, MEATHEAD. IT'S NOT DONE, AND WE DON'T PLAN WELL APART.COME HOME, BIG BROTHER.*

Kathy knew all the right things to say to address all his concerns. He would go home, but he didn't think it would help. The one person that had showed him how to live had just walked out of his life.

*I'M COMING.*

*GOOD. MOPE ON THE WAY. BE READY TO PLAN WHEN YOU GET HERE.*

# CHAPTER 19

*I*t took less than two days for Gloria to realize she had made a mistake. Knowing that you made a mistake doesn't mean you can go fix it either. For some reason, the natural reaction to knowing you've majorly messed up is crying.

Gloria cried. She cried because she had been afraid, and she realized now that she had been looking for any occasion to jump on to have an argument. She cried because Reid had no idea why she had gone so far to the right. Now that she was passed the crying phase, she was in the blaming stage. She blamed herself for letting her fear get the best of her.

Gloria was trying to avoid everyone. There was no way to explain she had thrown away the best thing in her life because of what she couldn't even tell you.

"Hey, what are you doing home? Aren't you supposed to be planning something? "Jack asked.

"We broke up," Gloria said.

"I'm sorry. I thought you were happy with him."

"Well, I don't know what I was with him. Now it doesn't matter because it's over."

"I'm not happy that it fell through. I was starting to like the guy. Maybe he wasn't the one, but he was able to show you that you can be in one. He showed you that you are ready."

Gloria nodded, and then turned the topic to mundane items. She needed to stop thinking about Reid. After the way she acted, there was no going back to what they had. Even knowing that she wanted to see Reid. She wanted to hear his laugh and be in his arms one last time.

The weekend came, and Gloria was sure she was going to hole up in her room. She might have gotten away with it if she didn't have Portia as a best friend. Portia came over unannounced and unapologetic.

"The worst thing you can do is stay home and try to figure out what happened in the relationship. What you need to do is use the positives from this experience. What you know now is that you are one hot woman. We know you are ready for the market, and we know that there are some trust issues but now that we know what they are, we know we can address them or at the very least we can head them off at the pass."

Portia decided it was time to buy some clothes, and so she and Gloria went hunting for some clothes that would make them feel way better. As usual, Portia had impeccable taste, but Gloria's mind kept going back to Reid. She was wondering what he was doing in his starter home. Was he even still here? When Gloria's engagement in the events seemed to be lagging, Portia recruited Jack, who was less than pleased to be taking off from his business. His concession was they needed to go to a store that sold some serving equipment he desperately needed. They went to a place in the mall called The Serving Spoon. The Serving Spoon had what Jack was looking for, and next to it was a dessert shop.

The shop was called The Tasty Bite. Portia pulled everyone in.

"Come along. We can all do with a little bit of sugar," Portia said.

"I don't know. Isn't the sugar just going to give me a temporary high, and then I'll come crashing down faster than before?" Gloria asked.

Portia looped her arm through her friend's as they walked into the dessert shop.

"Now the plan is when you start to fall, me or your brother will find a way to whack your spirits up. It's the aggressive shots of happiness that fend off the thinking of other things."

Gloria looked at Portia and realized that Portia had been here before.

"Portia, I'm so sorry. I should have been a better friend to you. To think you are going through something. I want you to know you can come to me. I'm here and whatever I have is yours."

Portia stopped, and for a moment Gloria thought that she was going to cry, but then Portia smiled and said, "Kiss, kiss, my love."

"Thank you. You are turning out to be my best friend ever."

"I'm sure there are better but thank you. So, we are going to get a dessert in the happy month of October. Maybe they will have the scary desserts out now."

Gloria went into the cute store, and instead of October commercialism in the windows there were several desserts that were in the shape of hearts and love. Just what Gloria didn't need to see. She knew what love was, and she had thrown it away. The rest of the day passed by, and Gloria couldn't wait to get back to her room. She had sent the final report to Grayson, and he had nothing but praise for it. Gloria wanted to reach out to Reid and ask him if he wanted to go over it, basically to find any excuse to see him to see if it was fixable.

Could she swallow her pride and reach out to him first?

*ARE YOU OKAY?*

Gloria sent the text and immediately wanted to pull it back. What kind of silly text was that? She waited for an hour and then put her phone on the dresser. There was no sense in torturing herself. Then her phone pinged. She had a text. Gloria was scared to look at it. Determined to not let fear guide her, she grabbed the phone and looked at the response.

*NO*

He had to be kidding. Was that all he was going to say? Gloria thought on it and wondered what else she expected him to say. At the end of the day, this wasn't his fault. She needed to pull herself together and just tell him what happened. Gloria needed to tell him that she was in love with him. She needed to tell him that she wanted to settle down with him on his horse farm. She wanted to have children and do the things that other people did. She just wasn't sure she was enough compared to the life he lived now. Reid did new things and traveled. Would he want to give that up for her? He had proposed, but was she going to be another company he had?

Then the phone pinged again.

*GRAYSON IS HAVING A FUNDRAISER. CAN YOU COME? SAME LOCATION AS LAST.*

*I'LL BE THERE.*

Why couldn't she have used her words rather than making those wild accusations? More importantly, their love was so quick Gloria was concerned that it wouldn't stick. These were all excuses of fear, and she wasn't going to live this way. Tomorrow would be a new day and a new way!

Reid's whole life would be decided tonight. He'd gone over the plan with Kathy, and she'd agreed that it was good but none of it mattered until Gloria got here. The room was full because everyone loved coming to a fundraiser by Grayson. Reid looked until he saw her in a black sheath dress.

As Gloria walked by, she caused a ruckus and didn't even know it. It was the way her hair was hanging down her back. She looked like a goddess walking around the room. Her hair was held back over her ears by delicate hair combs that looked like they had flowers coming out of the combs themselves, giving her an ethereal look. As if she could sense Reid, she turned and walked to him.

"Reid?"

"Gloria."

"Reid, I'm sorry. Why are you here?"

Reid smiled. "I accept your apology."

Gloria started speaking first, and he could barely

hear. "I was scared, and I want us to talk it through…"

Reid watched her eyes blink, and he stepped closer to run his hand up her shoulder. Then she stepped closer to him.

"I'm still scared, but I want to do this love thang with you. I love you, and we'll figure it out."

Reid looked at Gloria and once again felt confirmation that she was the most compassionate and sweetest woman in the world.

"I am very happy that you want to be with me, but I have been working with Kathy and I have a plan that I'm sure will work for us."

He could see the sparkle in her eye.

"You worked on this plan? "

"Yes, and I wanted to show you it's about us and no one else. First this," he said and gave her an envelope.

"What is this?"

"This is a folder on everything about me."

Gloria looked at him and began to blink quickly.

"I don't need this, Reid"

"I know you don't need it, but I want you to feel like we are on equal ground. Don't cry on me, Gloria. I want a life with you."

Gloria reached out her hand to Reid's cheek. "I love you crazy."

"Well, before you profess your undying love to me, I want you to know I'm going to shift the company work to Kathy and we will spend more time on the farm. I'd like you spend your time with me building up the farm to help therapy clients."

"Yes, yes, yes!" Gloria threw herself into his arms. Then she leaned back and kissed him. "Yes,

I'll take it and you. By the way did you still want to get married?"

Reid smiled. "Kathy is thinking a Christmas wedding will be fine."

Reid pulled Gloria in for another kiss and knew she was the one he had been waiting for.

# EPILOGUE

*V*incent Chance was in trouble.

He was always extremely practical. At one point, he thought that his brothers were just as practical. However, they'd all been finding women to love, and now the rules that made so much sense to him before and to them, for that matter, had been kicked to the side.

Love was a four-letter word that always seemed to cost someone something. Sitting at the mock rehearsal for Grayson and Rose's wedding, Vincent considered that maybe he was wrong. Grayson and Rose were going to have a wedding around Thanksgiving so that Gloria and Reid could have a wedding around Christmas.

Love and the holidays. It seemed as though those two afflictions went hand in hand. For him thanksgiving was the time people submitted the most proposals for him to review and on Christmas he took the time send out thank you cards to the private investigators and other personnel that helped him uncover shady partners before he committed to them. It was the season all right. The season to be grateful to others. He knew his brothers didn't share his thoughts on the season, but they would. According to Vincent, you stay in love forever.

Everywhere he turned, he saw people in relationships. It wasn't for him. He couldn't understand how his adopted brothers could forget the lessons of the past. How could they not remember that the reason they were brothers was that someone's love had turned fickle.

Sitting in the festive hall, the walls were decorated with printed flowers that were large and ripe hinting at the hopeful fertility and happiness of all who entered. Even the tables had a bouquet on every table so that some unlucky woman could take it home. In Vincent's mind it would be even worse if some unlucky guy had to take it home.

"Vincent, why are you here in the corner?" Reid asked with Gloria next to him. Vincent had been avoiding these two. If he understood correctly, it was his report that caused the initial rift. Although, it was the report he gave to Reid that also solved the issue Vincent didn't think a lot of people remembered that.

"I'm waiting to be told where to go stand and what to do," he grumbled.

Gloria went to Vincent and sat next to him.

"Maybe you want to do a little yoga with me. We can do some basic moves to relieve your stress."

Vincent shook his head right away.

"No, thank you. I don't know how you do it, but I see a lot of people in your classes and when they come out, they look a lot of things, like sweaty, exhausted, and beat up, but I wouldn't say anyone of those would be stress-free."

Vincent had to admit that Rose and Gloria were gems in their own right. They could pass the background search and they were amongst the last of their kind. When Vincent thought of the word "kind" he meant a woman who wanted a man for him and not for his net worth.

Gloria laughed and patted him on the shoulder.

"The offer stands, Vincent."

"When is the girl I'm partnered with, going to be here?"

Gloria and Reid looked around.

"She's coming. She had to take care of her child; I think. We'll be practicing without her. Don't worry, you're a genius. I'm sure you will be able to manage walking down the aisle with the bridesmaid."

www.ingramcontent.com/pod-product-compliance
Lightning Source LLC
Chambersburg PA
CBHW020122180626
46812CB00006B/2704